Sunrise City

Sunrise City

By

Rodney Riesel

Published by Island Holiday Publishing

East Greenbush, NY

ISBN: 978-0-9971149-6-6

First Edition

Special thanks to:

Pamela Guerriere

Kevin Cook

Cover Photo by:

Kim Seng at RoyalStockPhoto.com

Cover Design by:

Connie Fitsik

To learn about my other books friend me at

https://www.facebook.com/rodneyriesel

For Brenda,
Kayleigh, Ethan
& Peyton

Chapter One

I always thought Evan Walsh was an asshole. I thought he was an asshole even when we were kids. He was two grades behind me all the way through school so I just ignored him most of the time. There was just something about him that always rubbed me the wrong way. Most everyone else seemed to get along with him just fine, but anytime he was around, he just bugged the shit out of me. Come to think about it, it wasn't just something about him—it was *everything* about him. He had this weird way of walking up on his tiptoes. He spoke through his nose in a brassy, honking kind of voice like fingernails being dragged across a chalkboard. The sound made me want to blow chunks. I don't know, I guess I was the only one who noticed.

I graduated high school in '85 and went away to college for two years. I returned to Fort Pierce in '88 and joined the police department. And in '95 I married the love of my life.

From '85 to 2003 I never once thought about Evan Walsh. Then one day I was out in my front yard pushing the mower around and sweating my nutsack off, when my wife, Lynn, pulled into the driveway; she had just come from the gym. She was smiling when she got out of the car.

I stopped, shut off the lawnmower, and wiped the sweat from my forehead with the back of my hand. "What are you grinning about?" I asked.

Lynn had a towel draped around her shoulders and used the end of it to wipe her face. She was just as sweaty as I was, only I got that way for free whereas Lynn paid for a gym membership that she only used three or four times a month. Spending money wisely was never her strong point.

She chuckled a little when I asked her why she was smiling, and then proceeded to tell me about June, the girl—Lynn was thirty-three at the time, but still referred to herself and other women her age as girls—she had met at the gym. So, for the next few months it was June this, and June that, and "June is so funny" and "You would really like June."

I didn't know what was so funny about June, or why I would like her so much, because honestly, most times Lynn was talking about her I wasn't paying attention.

It was nothing new: Lynn had had these relationships before. It was nice when she had a friend, someone to pal around with. It was the next step where things usually took a turn for the worse ... not for Lynn or her new friend, but for me.

About three months into the relationship, what I knew was coming—what I feared was coming—came. We were sitting at the dinner table. Lynn had made chicken, Stove

Top stuffing, and canned green beans. Allison, our oldest daughter, sat to my right; she was eight years old at the time. Next to her was her little sister, Angel; she was five. Our son, C. J., which stood for Cole Jr.—named after me, of course—hadn't been born yet. Lynn was sitting at the other end of the table.

I was just about to scoop some Stove Top out of the old Corelle dinnerware bowl when Lynn said, "June's husband is in real estate."

"Oh, yeah?" I said.

"Yeah. He's really nice. I think you'd like him. His name is Evan."

I took a deep breath. *Here we go again,* I thought. I knew what was coming next.

"We should all do something together," Lynn said. "June and I were thinking dinner, maybe."

I could tell from Lynn's voice that she feared asking the question as much as I feared knowing she was eventually going to ask it.

"So, do you want to go to dinner with them this weekend?" she asked.

It was a good thing I never carried my revolver to the dinner table, because I might have shot myself in the head right at that moment. "I guess," I sighed.

"Don't act so enthused," Lynn said.

"I'll try not to." And then, like a giant lightning bolt made from human shit, it hit me. June's last name was Walsh. *Fuck!*

Over the next year and a half Lynn and I went out to dinner and to the movies with June and Evan maybe a dozen times or more; I hated every minute of it. I only did it for Lynn. Evan was still just as annoying as ever. Maybe even more so.

Right at the end of '03 our son, Cole Jr., was born, and a few months later, somewhere around the middle of 2004, Lynn and I separated, and soon after, divorced.

On the upside, since I considered June and Evan *her* friends, I never had to see Evan Walsh again.

Like I said, I always thought Evan Walsh was an asshole. I thought he was an asshole when we were kids, I thought he was an asshole years later when Lynn dragged him back into my life, and I thought he was an asshole as I held his hand in the hospital and watched him take his last breath.

I've never felt guilty for not liking someone, but that changes when you're standing above them watching them choke on their own blood and listening to the gurgling sound of air leaking through the holes in their chest.

Evan and I stared into each other's eyes as alarms rang out, hospital personnel hollered, and doctors and nurses shoved needles into his arms.

"You have to leave the room, Mr. Ballinger!" one nurse shouted at me.

I didn't move. I knew there was nothing they could do for Evan. I figured holding his hand was about the best thing anyone could do for him. I knew it was the least *I* could do.

I thought about all the times I rolled my eyes, or made a face when he said something stupid. I wondered if he had noticed. I wondered if he knew exactly how I felt about him. At that moment, I hoped he didn't. I hoped he thought he was holding his good friend's hand.

His chest rose slightly for the last time, and in that goddamn annoying voice of his, he forced out the words, "I'm sorry."

The bastard apologized for always being an asshole. I think he did it just to make me feel guilty. It did. *What an asshole*.

His grip loosened and I laid his arm on the bed next to him.

It got really quiet all of a sudden.

"Twelve-oh-six," one of the doctors said.

I looked down at the front of my shirt, it was covered in Evan's blood; so was my cargo shorts, and the tops of my flip-flops. In my twenty-five years with the Fort Pierce Police Department I had seen lakes blood like the one that gushed out of Evan before. It's something you never get used to. A few years back, when I retired, I hoped I would never see something like that again. I guess I just wasn't that lucky.

Chapter Two

I purchased The Breakwater Grill in 2013, the same year I retired from the police department. The Breakwater is a beachfront bar and restaurant that sits at the end of Seaway Drive, directly across from Jetty Park in Fort Pierce, Florida. It looks like every other beachfront bar in Florida. The walls are painted blue, there's a huge plastic marlin hanging on the wall, there's a few fishing nets, and a lobster trap on another wall. The floors are light brown ceramic tile with dark brown grout, and the ceiling is an old Armstrong drop ceiling I painted black when I bought the place.

I sunk my life savings into the place—well, half my life savings; I gave the other half away when I got divorced—and then borrowed the rest. At this point the place does a little better than break even. Luckily, I get to keep half of my retirement every month. The other half, of course, goes to my ex, who then brags about raising three children on her own in the house I paid for.

I stood behind the bar with my foot up on the bar sink and my elbow resting on my knee. "I don't know what you want from me, Lynn," I said into the phone. I hadn't spoken with Lynn in six weeks—since Evan's funeral—and even then we just nodded and said, "Hey."

Lynn and I don't speak that much these days; there's no need to. The girls are young adults and C. J. is fourteen. When we do speak, it's on the phone at the bar; I never gave Lynn my cell phone number, and the kids were asked not to give it to her either. Petty? Yes. But my cell phone is my last refuge. It's just nice to know that when it rings I might not know who's calling me, but I sure as hell know who isn't.

"I'm not a cop anymore, Lynn," I said. I glanced up at the two old bikers sitting at the bar. They were staring at me with smirks on their bearded faces. They didn't even know me, but they knew who I was talking to. All men can tell. I rolled my eyes and one of them laughed silently; his shoulders and belly shook.

"Fine, I'll ask around," I agreed reluctantly. I looked at the wall clock across from the bar. "No, I haven't seen her yet today. It's not even noon, Lynn." Now she was doing what she always did in phone conversations. Once we were done discussing the topic at hand, she brought the kids into the conversation. I never figured out if she does this to annoy me or just to keep me on the phone a little longer.

"I gotta go," I said. "Yeah … yeah … yeah … bye." I hung up the phone and took a deep breath.

"Ex?" one of the bikers asked.

"Yeah," I grumbled.

He slid his empty beer mug across the bar toward me, the condensation leaving a long wet streak behind it. "Can I get another one ah those?"

I grabbed his mug, held it under the Blue Moon tap and pulled the lever.

The biker pulled his black leather billfold from his back pocket and peered inside. He walked his fingers through the bills and pulled out two tens. "Get one fer yourself," he said, tossing the bills on the bar. "I know I can always use a drink after talking to my ex."

"Thanks," I said.

"Luckily she's only allowed to call him on Sundays between noon and three," the second biker added.

"Court order?" I asked, half joking.

"More or less," the first guy said. "She's up in Lowell on a manslaughter charge."

"You mean *woman* slaughter," the second guy said with a chuckle.

I pulled myself a Coors Light and set the glass on the bar in front of me. I always drink Coors Light when I'm behind the bar. It's a lot like drinking club soda, only with a nastier taste, but it never seems to fill you up, and if you drink it slow enough, you never seem to get drunk. My buddy, Kelly Morgan, always says, "Whenever you drink a Coors Light you have to turn around quick and lick your own asshole to get the taste out of your mouth."

"You ready for another?" I asked the second guy.

He tilted his glass slightly and inspected the contents. "I'm good for now," he replied.

The door on the east side—the ocean side—of the building opened and in walked two thirty-somethings. She was short with long brown hair pulled back into a pony-tail, and wearing a hunter green bikini. He was tall and skinny with no muscle tone at all and wore white board shorts with a palm tree down one leg. He was also wearing a red tank top. On his left arm was a tattoo of a palm tree. Evidently he loved palm trees. The one-day-old sunburn told me they were either just visiting Florida, or they had entered a lobster look-a-like contest.

"Can I get a rum and Coke, and a Malibu and pineapple?" the kid asked. Everyone under forty is a kid to me now.

I didn't answer, I just reached into the well for the rum and began making the drinks. Talking with the ex that early in the day puts me in a bad mood.

"Can we take the drinks down to the beach?" the girl asked.

"Sure," I said. What the hell did I care?

I gave them their drinks and they gave me my money. *Cha-ching!* I'd be buying a boat and living on my own private island in no time.

Me and the bikers watched her ass as it wiggled across the floor and out the door.

"Good God," said the biker drinking the Blue Moon. "I'd pay her a hundred bucks if she'd let me strip down naked and then have her beat the shit outta me."

"That's someone's daughter, Frank," said the other guy.

"Every girl is somebody's daughter, Poco," Frank replied.

"Nude ass-kicking might be a health code violation," I added. They both laughed. Bikers always seem to have a great sense of humor.

Poco looked at his wrist watch. "Is it almost lunch time?" he asked. "I'm so hungry I could eat a nun's ass through a convent gate."

That was one I had never heard before. I made a mental note to remember it.

"You serving lunch yet?" Frank asked.

"Sure are," I answered. I turned, grabbed two menus off the back bar, and handed one to each of them.

"Whatddaya recommend?" Poco asked.

I grabbed a guest pad from under the bar and tossed it on the bar top in front of me. "Grouper sandwich is good," I said.

"I'll have the grouper sandwich," said Poco. "And fries."

Frank closed his menu. "I guess I'll have the same thing."

I jotted their orders on a ticket and brought it to the kitchen.

"Order up!" I said.

Leon was sitting on a stool at the back of the kitchen peeling potatoes. He climbed off the stool and tossed the potato he was working on back in the white five-gallon bucket. "What do we got?" he asked.

"Two grouper sandwiches with fries."

On my way back to the bar I looked at the wall clock again. It was 12:25. *Where is she?* I wondered. *Her shift started at noon. Kids.*

The door that led to Seaway Drive—the door on the north side of the building—opened and in walked Allison, my oldest girl. "I know, I know," she said.

The bikers looked her over. I knew what they were thinking. The curse of being a man is knowing that we're all pigs, and knowing what we're all thinking. You just try to put it out of your mind. My old partner, Jim Canton, told me once—when Lynn was first pregnant—that when you have a son, you only have one prick to worry about, but when you have a daughter, you have everyone's prick to worry about. Looking back, a lot of wisdom came out of that man.

Allison is a pretty girl, twice as pretty as her mom was at that age, which was twenty-two. I guess that's what happens when you mix in the Ballinger genes. She's five-seven, three inches taller than her mom; she got that from me too—I'm six-three. Her hair is long, blond, and pin straight; that's from Lynn.

"Speaking of daughters," I said. Of course, I only announced it because I knew once they knew she was my daughter at least they wouldn't say anything out loud. Probably some unwritten guy code bullshit, but it worked for me.

Allison came behind the bar, tied her apron around her waist, and began texting ... you know, because that's what you do at work nowadays.

"You're supposed to leave that in your car," I informed her for the ten millionth time.

She pushed a button on top of the cell and it went dark. She stuffed it into the front pocket of her shorts—the shorts I had asked her not to wear to work because they were *too* short.

"What if someone needs to get a hold of me?" she replied.

"Like your agent, or your personal assistant?" I asked sarcastically.

"Daddy," she said. The kid has great comebacks.

After two years of begging, I finally started letting Allison work at the bar part-time. She's been here a little over six weeks now, and to tell you the truth I like spending time with her. It makes work into a kind of father/daughter project.

"Did you see your sister last night?" I asked.

Allison began filling the bar sink. "I haven't seen her since last Sunday."

"Has your mom heard from her?"

"She hasn't mentioned it."

As I left the bar I said, "Get these guys another drink, on me." I nodded. "Thanks for coming in, guys."

They nodded back. "Thank you," Poco said, and raised his glass.

I walked out the door that faces the water. To my right was an outdoor bar we used in the evenings. In front of me were plastic tables and chairs. Beyond those was a small stage for live music. I walked between the stage and the volleyball net, and down the sandy pathway that led to the beach.

I stood in the sand on a little hill that over-looked the water and pulled my cell phone from my pocket and dialed Angel's number. The smell of a skunk's ass filled my nostrils; and I jerked my head toward the three young girls sitting on beach towels and smoking a joint.

Hey! This is Angel. I'm far too busy to get to the phone but if you leave a message I'll probably ignore it. Beep!

"Angel, it's your father. Just wondering how you were doing. Haven't heard from you in a few days. Call me back. Love ya."

I stuck the cell phone back in pocket and looked back toward the potheads. As one girl handed the joint to the other, she paused and motioned it toward me.

What the hell, I thought. I don't smoke weed very often, but I'm not the kind of guy who turns it down either. I walked over, grabbed the joint, and took a much bigger drag than they had probably wanted me to. I held the smoke and said, "Thanks" as I handed it back to her. I exhaled. They giggled as I walked away.

I retrieved my cell from my pocket once again and dialed. "Can I speak to Detective Cooper?" I asked.

"Um, one second," said the woman at the other end.

A few seconds later a man came on the line. "Can I help you?" he asked.

"Coop?" I asked.

"Can I ask who's calling?"

"It's Cole Ballinger. I'm calling for Sid Cooper."

"Hey, Cole. It's Spence."

"Oh, how's things, Spence?"

"Good, Cole."

"Is Coop around?"

There was a short pause. "Sid passed away like a month ago, Cole. You hadn't heard?"

"Jesus Christ! What happened?"

"Heart attack. He dove into his pool at home. Never came up."

"Shit. He's three or four years younger than me."

"Is there anything I can help you with, Cole?"

It took me a second to remember why I called. "Oh … yeah, I was wondering how a murder investigation was going. I just had a few questions."

"Was it something Sid was working on?"

"Oh, I don't know who's got it. It was a stabbing that happened in a parking lot over on Indian River Drive."

"I can look into it and get back to you."

"Thanks a lot, Spence. I would really appreciate that."

"Uh, Allison still working at the bar?"

"Yes, Spence," I replied. "Why don't you stop in later? She would probably love to see you."

"Hey, maybe I will."

Spence was a good kid. Made detective at twenty-nine years old. Spence is the type of guy every father wishes their daughter would marry. That's why I figured it couldn't hurt to have him around. Girls never date the guys their fathers like.

Chapter Three

Detective Spence Oller walked into The Breakwater Grill two days later; Saturday afternoon, around three. He was dressed in a light gray sports coat and matching pants. His black dress shoes were shined to perfection and not one dirty blond hair on his head was out of place. He let the door close behind him and removed his Wayfarers. When his eyes adjusted to the darkness of the room he proceeded on to the bar, scanning the room as he moved. I knew he was looking for Allison; her shift had ended two hours earlier. Too bad, Spence.

"What can I get ya, Spence?" I sang out.

He loosened his tie. "I'll, ah, just have a ginger ale. Thanks, Cole." he said as his blue eyes swept the bar area.

"You lose something, Spence?" I asked, as I shot ginger ale from the soda gun into a red plastic cup. I set the cup in front of him and grabbed a straw. For most adults I would have poured the soda into a glass and stuck a lime or lemon wedge on the rim, but this was Spence and I thought it would be funnier if I let him believe I saw him as just another kid.

"Lose something?" he parroted absently, eyes still searching like a spotlight.

"Yeah. You keep looking around the room like you lost something."

"She left two hours ago," came Melvin Mulhern's grumbly old voice from the end of the bar. Melvin was in his mid-eighties, I think. He spent most days between noon and four at the bar. He was sitting at the end of the bar the day I took ownership, and he'll probably be here the day I'm lucky enough to hand the keys to the next poor bastard.

"Left? Who left?" Spence asked unconvincingly.

Whenever Melvin laughed—which is what he did when Spence asked the question—I got a little nervous. First his shoulders would start shaking, then he would let out this rattling wheeze, and then his whole body would turn blue. Every time he laughed I was sure he was going to die. The fact that he laughed at everything made matters worse. He was a miserable old bastard who was always laughing for no good reason. He was good for atmosphere and not much else. He creeped out some of my regulars—me, too, on occasion.

Spence sipped his soda. "I asked around about that stabbing, Cole," he said. "It wasn't Sid's case."

"Who's got it?" I asked.

"It's still on Franklin's desk but it's getting cold."

Franklin was Tommy Franklin. He had been on the job for around thirty years, twenty-one of those with a gold shield. He was a good detective. If the case was going cold, there was a good chance it wasn't Tommy's fault.

"What did you find out?" I asked.

"I told Franklin it was you asking. Hope that was okay."

"That's fine."

"He said the victim, Evan Walsh, was stabbed thirty-three times; mostly in the torso. There were a few defensive wounds on the hands, and arms."

I winced a little remembering the bloody scene in the hospital.

Spence continued. "There were no weapons found at the scene but the coroner says the wound pattern and angle of penetration shows there were two attackers."

"Huh. Any witnesses?"

"Not one. Uniforms canvassed the area and knocked on doors. No one heard or saw a thing."

"There was no one else in the parking lot?" I asked.

"The Subway—where he had purchased a sandwich—was the only business open that late, so the parking lot was empty. Security footage shows Walsh was the only one in the store minutes before the attack."

"What about the clerk?"

"He said he ran to the back of the store to use the restroom the second that Walsh left the store. When he came out of the bathroom—the restrooms are right next to the rear entrance—he saw the victim laying in the parking lot."

"So it was the clerk at Subway who phoned it in?"

"Right," Spence answered and took another sip through his bendy-straw. He pulled out his wallet and laid a five-dollar bill on the bar to pay for his drink.

I held up my hand. "I got his one, Spence."

"You never bought *me* a goddamn drink," Melvin grumbled.

"What have you ever done for me?" I shot back.

"I come into this shit hole every day and buy your watered-down booze, that's what I do. It's people like me who keep this place going."

"You come in here and nurse two drinks, sometimes one, the whole time you're here. I doubt that's what keeps me open."

"I can only *have* two. I have to drive home, ya know."

"They shouldn't even allow your sorry old ass in a car when you're *sober*. Much less after two drinks."

"Fuck you, you ungrateful bastard," Melvin hollered.

I laughed and then Melvin laughed. He lived through that one too.

Chapter Four

The following evening around six I pulled my red, 2009 Ford F-150 into the driveway at 1104 Weatherbee Road. I shut off the engine and thought for a second. How long has it been since I was here last? The day Allison graduated high school. Wow! Five years.

The palm trees that ran along each side of the driveway—the ones I planted back in '97—were a little taller. The house had been painted. It used to be light beige, now it was a light brown. The mailbox was different. The old one was black and metal and sat atop a treated four-by-four. The new one was one of those shitty one-piece green plastic mailboxes.

As I walked up the driveway toward the front door I wondered who had painted the house and installed the mailbox. None of my business, I guess. It wasn't my house anymore.

I rang the doorbell and a few seconds later Lynn opened the door. She smiled, I didn't. I figured I'd do my smiling when she started sending *me* half of *her* retirement every month.

"Cole, it's nice to see you," Lynn said. Her voice had a surprised tone, as though she hadn't known I was coming.

"Lynn," I said.

"Come in." She turned and walked down the hallway toward the kitchen. I looked around as I followed her to see what other home improvements I had paid for. There was nothing obvious.

"I just made coffee," she informed me. "Would you like a cup?"

"Sure."

Lynn motioned toward one of the stools that sat at a bar separating the kitchen from the dining room. "Sit."

I took a seat and wondered if she was going to say "Good boy," but she didn't. She poured us each a coffee in matching blue mugs. The mugs were much too large for evening coffee. I figured she was remembering back to when I would doze off while she was speaking, and thought the coffee might keep me awake.

After the coffee was poured she said, "Still have it black?"

"Yeah."

She opened a cupboard over the sink and grabbed a half empty bottle of Jameson. There were a few other bottles of booze in the cabinet as well. "You want a shot in yours?" she asked.

"No, thanks," I replied.

Lynn dumped a shot and a half into hers. "It'll help me sleep later. Sure you won't have one?"

I wanted one, all right. "No, thanks."

She replaced the bottle and shut the cabinet door. She set my mug in front of me and hers on the countertop in front of her; she stood in the kitchen opposite me. "So, where were we?" she asked.

"Nowhere," I answered.

Lynn blew into her coffee and had a small sip. "It's good, isn't it? The coffee, I mean."

"I haven't tasted it yet."

"I got it at that coffee place over by the marina. Have you been there yet?"

"No." I cautiously took a sip of the coffee so as not to burn my lip.

"Good, isn't it?" Lynn asked again.

"You seem awful damn eager for my opinion."

"Just making conversation."

"Okay, yeah, it's good." I looked around. "Is C.J. here?"

"He's at a friend's house," Lynn replied.

"Did you tell him I was coming over?"

"No. I thought it would be better if we spoke alone."

"I would have liked to see him."

"Are you trying to start a fight?"

Here we go. "No," I replied.

"I just thought it would be better if we didn't talk about a murder in front of our fourteen-year-old son."

And we sure wouldn't want him to witness one, I thought. "I didn't see him at the funeral."

"He didn't go. Allison went, but I told C.J. he was probably too young for something like that. He's never been to a funeral before and I figured his first one shouldn't be someone so close."

"I didn't realize you and June were still close."

"We still see each other a few times a year." Lynn's eyes drifted off toward the sliding glass door that overlooked the pool. "We're not as close as we used to be."

"Have you seen her since the funeral?" I asked.

"Just once. I stopped over the morning I spoke with you on the phone ... Thursday morning."

"And she asked you to call me?"

"No. I did that on my own. She was telling me that the case was going nowhere. The detective told her there were no leads and no suspects ... no witnesses. I felt terrible for her. I thought maybe if I called you there would be something you could do."

"I called and asked about it. Tommy Franklin has it. Remember Tommy?"

She nodded yes.

"He's good at his job," I assured her. "But June was right, there's no suspects yet. No witnesses. There was no weapon found. They don't really have much to go on. There's really not anything more I can do."

"Well, I just thought—"

"I'll give him a call in a few days and see if anything has changed."

Lynn reached out and put her hand on mine. "Thanks, Cole," she said.

I pulled my hand back. "I gotta get going. Tell C.J. I was here."

"I will."

I walked back to my truck, and as I backed out of the driveway and headed down the road I thought about Lynn's hand on mine. I remembered how good it made me feel, years ago, when she touched me, and I thought about how it only angered me today. It wasn't just the money, the child support, the retirement. Money's just money. The grudge I still carried was the way she robbed me of being a full-time father. The girls and I were close. We did everything together, went everywhere together. I tucked them into their beds every night and read them stories that ended with *happily ever after*. And then one day a wife and a judge decided that being a full-time father was no longer my right. Lynn had been awarded full custody of the children, with me having limited visitation privileges. "You're lucky you'll get to see you kids so often—every other weekend," the judge had informed me.—Some fathers don't have that privilege."

Privilege, my ass. It was cruel punishment for a crime I hadn't committed.

My argument at the time was, "Lynn works nights. I'm home with the kids almost every night. I fix their dinner, I give them their baths, I put them in bed at night. The kids are in school or at daycare during the day, when Lynn's home. She rarely sees them. She didn't even want children. It was me, I wanted the kids." The judge just gave me the old I've-heard-that-story-before look. He didn't give a shit; he was going home to *his* children that night.

Allison was nine and Angel was six at the time of the divorce. Allison took it a lot better than Angel. C.J. was just a baby, so he never knew any different. What might have been, I wonder, every time I'm with one of my kids. What would our relationships be if things had remained the same? Would their lives be better? Allison and C.J. seemed fine but maybe Angel would have stayed in school. Maybe I wouldn't get a call in the middle of the night from an old cop friend who recognized her last name. Maybe I wouldn't have to go into an old abandoned crack house and pick Angel up in my arms off a piss-soaked mattress and carry her out to my truck. I didn't even ask Lynn about Angel while I was there. It would have only started a fight.

Put her hand on mine. Fuck her!

Chapter Five

Allison was only late by a half hour on Monday morning.

"You missed your boyfriend the other day," Melvin told her.

Allison didn't look up from her intense texting session. "My boyfriend?" she asked. "Who's my boyfriend?"

"That skinny cop with all the grease in his hair," Melvin replied.

"That's gel, Mr. Mulhearn."

"Yeah, well, it don't gel with me. Am I gonna get a drink or what?" Melvin looked at his wrist watch. "I've been sitting here for an hour."

"Mr. Mulhearn, you got here after me and I've only been here for ten minutes."

"Time drags when the glass is empty, princess. And stop calling me Mr. Mulhearn. My father is Mr. Mulhearn."

"You mean your father *was* Mr. Mulhearn," I said as I passed behind him carrying a five-gallon pail of ice.

"Was?" said Melvin. "My old man ain't dead, ya know."

Allison and I both cocked our heads. "Your father's still alive?" I asked.

"Yeah. I just had Sunday dinner with him yesterday."

I hoisted the bucket of ice up onto the bar top. "How the hell old is *he*?"

"Ninety-nine. He'll be one hundred at the end of the year."

"Does he live with you?" Allison asked.

"Hell no. He's got his own place in White City. Can't have some old man like that living with me. It would cramp my style. What if I wanted to bring a woman home?"

I snorted and said good-naturedly, "Why the hell would a dried-up old fart like you bring a woman home? What would you do with her when you got her there?"

Melvin put a finger to his lips and nodded toward Allison. "Not in front of the little girl," he said, shushing me.

"Is your mother still alive?" Allison asked.

Melvin leaned back luxuriously. I could tell he was eating up all this attention. "Never knew my mother, princess," he said. "The way my old man tells it, he was fifteen and she was seventeen. She was a Cuban girl; her family worked for my grandparents. She got pregnant, and after I was born her and her family moved away. My grandparents kept me. Later, after my old man graduated from college and got a job, I came down to live with him. Only saw my grandparents once after that. Never saw my mother again. Oh, I had a couple step-moms along the way, but none I would call my mother." Melvin paused for a second. "And I guess that brings us right up to the point where I'm still sitting here without a drink."

"Oh, sorry." Allison spun around and grabbed a rocks glass off the counter. She filled it with ice, poured in a shot of well Scotch, and dropped a lemon wedge inside. "There you go, Mr. Mul—Melvin."

"Thanks, princess," said Melvin.

"That one's on me," I said.

Melvin sat up straight and puffed out his chest. "Well, well, well, big suspender. If I hadda known all I had to do was tell my life story to get a free drink, I woulda done it a long time ago. Maybe next time I'll tell you about my first wife dying of cancer; might get me a free lunch."

I shook my head. "You're a real asshole, Melvin."

"Takes one to know one," he laughed.

Me and Allison froze in our spots waiting for him to catch his breath. Waiting … waiting … waiting … and, he's good.

"Pour me a Coors Light," I said.

Allison poured the beer and handed me the glass. I went into the kitchen to make sure Leon was ready to serve the lunch crowd. He was. He was always ready. He always got to work on time—an hour or so before me—and he was always a great worker. Maybe the best employee I ever had. It almost makes me feel bad that I once had to arrest him. I even feel worse that I once had to shoot him.

"How's everything going back here, Leon?" I asked as the kitchen door slammed shut behind me.

"Good, boss," Leon replied.

Leon always called me boss, even back when I was a cop, and he was a piece of shit muscle for a loan shark who went by the name of Choctaw Dave. Choctaw Dave's grandparents came here from Ireland in the thirties. Dave had red hair and was the color of notebook paper. Who knows where the Choctaw nickname came from? After Choctaw Dave went to prison, Leon switched over to breaking and entering. It's been about twenty years since I shot Leon. He did a ten-year stint in Raiford after that. He's stayed out of trouble ever since … as far as I know. And evidently, he doesn't hold a grudge, which I'm grateful for, because Leon could beat the average man to death with his bare hands. I didn't want to be that man.

"You need me to do anything?" I asked. I always asked, and I always hoped he said no. I'm lazy; I've always been lazy. I became a cop because it was easy, not because of the old bullshit story about wanting to help people. Being a cop today *isn't* easy. I wouldn't want to be a cop today. I got in at the right time, and retired at the right time—just before YouTube's main function became busting cops' balls. In my day no one jammed a cell phone in your face while you tried to do your job, thank God.

"No, I'm good," Leon said. Good man, Leon. Good man.

The kitchen door that led to the alley between my place and the Bluewater Grill swung open, and in came Kelly Morgan pushing a hand truck filled with cases of

Bud Light. His red Budweiser shirt was soaked with sweat. He was wearing navy-blue cargo shorts, black sneakers, and black ankle socks. He placed his foot on the axle and eased the hand truck forward, placing the six cardboard cases in the middle of the kitchen floor.

"Hot out there?" I asked, and then took a big swig of my Coors Light.

"Not hot enough to drink that shit," he replied.

"This coming from a man who drinks lime-flavored beer."

Kelly wiggled the hand truck out from under the cases and returned to his truck for another load. I picked up one of the cases and took it to the walk-in cooler. I usually try to plan it so I walk into a room after the work is done, and then ask if anyone needs any help.

I had carried three boxes into the cooler by the time Kelly returned with six more—two Bud Lights and four Bud Heavies.

"Those first six should have been gone when I got back with these," Kelly jabbed.

"Last stop?" I asked.

"Two more. You sticking around?"

"I would imagine."

"I'll stop back by." He glanced over at Leon and then back at me. He motioned his head toward the door and went out. I followed.

When we got the rear of his side loader he turned to me and said, "Hey, I didn't want to say anything in front of Leon, but I saw Angel at my last stop."

"Where?" I asked.

"I was at the CVS on the corner of White City Road and Route 1. She was in the parking lot of the liquor store next door. I hollered her name, she looked back, and then climbed into a car with two guys—black guy and a white guy."

"Get a plate number?"

"No, it was too far away. It was a Plymouth Duster, '73 or '74, maybe. Brown. A beat-up old piece of shit."

"Recognize the guys she was with?"

"No."

"How did she—never mind, I know how she looked." I scratched my head with both hands. "Fuck."

"Sorry, Cole."

"Don't be sorry. Thanks for letting me know."

Kelly slapped me on the back as I turned back toward the bar. "I'll stop back in an hour or so. We'll have a drink."

"And a stogie," I added.

It was around one-thirty by the time Kelly got back to the bar. I had walked out to the beach with my second beer of the day, and was now staring out at the ocean holding an empty bottle. I spent most of the time between Kelly leaving and getting back thinking about Angel. I hadn't told Allison that Kelly had seen her. And I quickly figured out—from speaking with Allison—that Lynn hadn't told her or C.J. that I'd been out to the house the day before. Gotta keep those secrets.

I spent most of the afternoon wondering how I could save Angel. What could we do for her? How could we help her? Her mother and I had recently stopped giving her money—the one thing we could agree on. That's probably why we hadn't seen her lately; we were of no use to her anymore. When she knew she could get money she would show up at the bar, or at her mother's house, with a story about needing money for rent, or food. The money we gave her always went for drugs. We finally decided that if we quit giving her money maybe she couldn't buy drugs. It never works out that way. Addicts always find a way to get what they need. Lie, cheat, steal, manipulate … whatever it takes.

Times like these—alone, thinking about Angel—I create scenarios in my head where I say just the right thing to her. And suddenly, in a moment of clarity, she opens her eyes and realizes what she's doing to herself, and to her family. I had been a cop long enough to know that would never happen. I knew the statistics. I knew where it was headed.

I watched a little girl, nine or ten, and her father play on the beach. He would throw a Frisbee to her; she rarely caught it. The little girl would then throw it back to him, never throwing it anywhere near him. He would jump and dive and try as hard as he could to catch that damn Frisbee. Not so she would think he was a great catcher, but so she would think she did a great job of throwing it. Every little girl looks at her father and sees Superman. I wonder if Angel ever wakes up covered in sweat in the stinking dark of some unknown drug house and has no idea where she is and wonders why Superman doesn't swoop in and save her. Superman really let her down.

I flinched when the cold rocks glass touched the back of my arm.

"Staring at that guy in the Speedo?" Kelly joked.

I grabbed the bourbon and Coke. "No. I like a guy with more hair on his back and a slightly larger belly."

We both sipped our drinks as we watched the fifty-something in the Speedo walk along the beach with a woman we hoped was his very attractive daughter, but probably wasn't.

"She seems to like him," Kelly pointed out.

"Yeah," I said. "And here we stand womanless."

"It's probably because we're *too* good-looking."

"Unapproachable," I added.

"Yeah, that's it." Our heads slowly turned when a young brunette in a purple thong walked by. "If they'd just get to know us," I sighed.

"Stogie?" I said when the young woman passed by.

"Sure," Kelly replied. We turned and headed back toward the bar.

Kelly sat at one of the picnic tables near the volleyball nets. I went on inside and grabbed two cigars I was keeping behind the bar—two five-inch Don Lugos.

"Grab me that lighter, Allison," I said, pointing at the cheap purple Bic knock-off lying on the back bar.

Melvin had left and Allison had cleared away his glass. Three late-twenty-something guys sat at the bar, each wearing swim trunks, flip-flops, and T-shirts.

Allison handed me the lighter.

"How's everything going?" I asked.

"Good," she said.

I went back out to the picnic tables, biting the tip off my cigar and spitting it into the sand as I walked. I tossed Kelly's cigar on the table in front of him and then lit my own. I slowly spun the cigar in my mouth and inhaled as I held the flame to the end. When the entire tip glowed red I exhaled, removed it from my mouth, and blew on it. Kelly lit his own with pretty much the same bravado.

We sat on the same bench with our backs against the table sipping our drinks and smoking our cigars. We commented on the weather. We joked about the rough lifestyle we lived in Florida. We talked about booze and each told a story about getting drunk as a kid. Kelly told the one about severing a telephone pole with an old F-150, and I told the one about passing out with my head wedged between two pickets of a four-foot fence. We had told the stories before, but that didn't matter; guys could never tell those stories too many times. Then we didn't say anything for a while.

"Daddy!" Allison shouted from the doorway.

My head snapped around. Feeling the urgency in her voice, I stood.

"Daddy, Angel just called!" she hollered.

I went toward the bar. Kelly stood and followed me.

"Is she okay?" I asked.

"She sounded pretty messed up. She was crying. She asked me if I could go pick her up."

"Where is she?"

"South Twenty-Eighth."

"She give a house number?"

"No. Can I go try to find her?" Allison asked.

"Definitely not." I pulled my cell from my pocket and dialed Angel's number. I got her voicemail. I tried again. Same thing.

"You want to take a ride?" Kelly asked.

I took a deep breath. "I guess." I turned back to Allison. "She say who she was with?"

"No." I thought about my .357 revolver locked in a metal box in my office. I thought about placing the end of the barrel against some crack dealer's forehead and turning his skull into a taco shell. Then I decided to leave the Smith and Wesson where it was.

Kelly's maroon-colored, dual cab Ford pickup was in a parking space on the other side of Jetty Park. We hurried across the street and through the park.

"South Twenty-Eighth Street?" Kelly asked, just to make sure.

"Yeah. Who knows where, though," I replied. I had been in that neighborhood many times as a cop. Images of each home ran through my mind as Kelly drove along Seaway Drive.

Twenty-Eight Street is less than twenty minutes from The Breakwater Grill, but when you're on your way to pick up your little girl at some shit hole drug den, it seems a lot longer.

Kelly swung a right onto Acorn Street and then veered right at Mississippi Avenue. We stopped at the end of Mississippi and took a left onto Twenty-Eighth. *Where is she?* I thought. I quickly tried her cell again. Voicemail.

Kelly maneuvered the big Ford slowly down the street while we inspected each home. I scanned the windows, the doors, the driveways, the front yards. Most of the modest one-story block homes were owned by working class families. There were nice cars in the driveways. Some had boats. The easiest way to find the house we were looking for would have been to knock on a door and ask where the neighborhood crack house was. They all knew where it was. Most of them had surely called the police at one time or another. Of course nothing was ever done because no one of any importance lived on their street. Drug houses get shut down a lot faster when they're in the neighborhood of a councilman, a cop, or any number of other city officials.

We got lucky. Kelly spotted the old Plymouth Duster he had seen earlier in the day parked in a driveway about four houses down from the corner, on the right. He pulled to the curb and shut off the engine. When I saw his hand reach for the door handle I said, "Wait here. I'll go in by myself."

"I'm not letting you walk into that place alone," he responded.

"I've done it before," I said, "and I'll probably do it again." I climbed out.

The salmon-colored one-story home had been sided long ago with four-by-eight sheets of what contractors call T1-11. Basically it's plywood that gives a reversed board and batten appearance. Several windows were broken and had been repaired with cardboard pizza boxes. I walked up the dirt pathway to the door. The main door was open but the screen door was locked. I guess you can't be too careful nowadays. You wouldn't want just *any* crack addict to walk in off the street. I pulled out a small pocket knife I kept in the lower pocket of my cargo shorts and made a six-inch slit in the fiberglass screen. I stuck my hand through the slice and unlocked the door. The smell—I can only describe as a mixture of piss, shit, harsh chemicals, and burnt plastic—hit me before I even pulled open the door.

I walked into the living room first. I paused to let my eyes adjust to the darkness. Three bare mattresses, black and greasy with the filth of untold bodies, were the only furniture. There were no pictures on the walls, and only one window had a curtain. A few spent syringes were scattered around the floor as well as an old broken crack pipe or two.

On one mattress a gaunt skeleton of a white male anywhere between fifteen and seventy—it was hard to tell—sat with his back against the wall. He had on the nastiest pair of Levis I'd ever seen. He was shirtless and wore no shoes or socks. His torso was tattooed with sores or burns, some fresh, some healed over into purplish scabs. As I walked across the floor toward the entrance to the hallway his head slowly turned in my direction. He stared through me, like he knew someone was there but just couldn't quite see them. I moved on down the hall like a ghost.

I pushed open the door of the first room I came to; a black man lay passed out on a nasty old sleeping bag encrusted with dried vomit and riddled with tears and burn holes. His foot was caught in one of the rips and white stuffing littered the room. He jerked in his stupor and let out a little yip, and then his body shook all over before coming deathly still again. A fresh pile of shit in the corner was already attracting flies and cockroaches *My daughter, in a place like this...*

I opened the second door. Angel was lying on the stained carpeting. She was wearing only a dingy bra and matching panties. Angel had lost a lot of weight since the last time I saw her. I could count her ribs from where I stood. She opened her eyes when she heard me enter the room. "Daddy," she whispered.

"It's okay, baby," I said. It wasn't okay.

I scanned the room for her clothing. I found a red sleeveless top and a pair of denim shorts. I didn't know if they were hers but I wanted her clothed when I brought her out.

She did her best to sit up, and I pulled the shirt over her head.

"I love you, Daddy," Angel said.

"I love you too, baby." I slid the shorts over her feet, pulled them up around her waist, and buttoned them. I helped her to her feet, put her arm around my neck. And we walked out of the room.

When we got to the living room, the shirtless guy was standing. "Hey," he said. "Where are you taking my girlfriend?"

I hit him hard in the throat with the back of my hand. He grabbed his neck and dropped to the floor. I hoped I would read in the paper the next morning about the crack addict who was found dead in some shit hole on South Twenty-Eighth Street.

I picked up my little girl and carried her to the truck.

Chapter Six

Kelly dropped Angel and me off at my apartment on Grand Club Place and then drove his truck back to the bar. He told me that he would have someone drive my truck to my place and drop it off.

I phoned Allison and told her what had happened, and that I probably wouldn't be back in. I told her Angel was fine and was sleeping. Then I called Norma Winkle.

Norma was fifty-seven years old. She had short brown hair with bangs cut about an inch above her brow line and a long nose that took a dive at the end. She looked a lot like a bald eagle. Norma had worked for me since the beginning; she had also worked for the bar's previous owner. She knew how the place ran better than I did, and if I had an assistant manager it would be her. I told Norma I had a little emergency, I wouldn't be in, and wondered if she could go in and cover for me, even though it was her night off. She said yes, of course, because that's the type of person Norma is.

Angel slept in the spare room the entire night. I sat in the hall next to the open door listening to her breath. Around four in the morning I went into the living room and fell asleep on the couch.

I made pancakes for breakfast, because they were Angel's favorite when she was a kid. I dumped the pancake mix into a plastic bowl and as I added the water, oil, and eggs I thought back to all the times I made pancakes for her and her sister.

It was around 10:00 am when Angel, still dressed in the clothes from the day before, stumbled down the hall and into the kitchen. She rubbed her eyes and looked at me.

"There's coffee there," I said, motioning toward the coffee pot.

She shook her head no.

"I made pancakes."

Angel placed the palm of her hand on her belly. "I don't think I could eat anything." She walked into the living room and sat on the couch. I guess pancakes aren't the magical life-changing meal I thought they were. It would have been nice if she sat down, bit into a pancake, and was instantly transformed back into the little princess she used to be.

"Do you have any 7Up, or ginger ale, or anything?" Angel asked. She stared at the TV. An old episode of *Unsolved Mysteries* was playing on Lifetime.

I glanced out the living room window to make sure my truck had found its way home. It had. "I can run and grab you some, if you want," I said.

Angel smiled. "Thanks, Daddy. That would be awesome." She picked a scab on her cheek as she spoke.

I slipped on my flip-flops and told her I would be right back.

My truck doors were unlocked and the keys were stashed over the visor. I drove to CVS and bought a two-liter of 7Up and another of ginger ale. I also grabbed some orange juice and a copy of the News Tribune. I scanned the headlines as I stood in the checkout line. Either no crack addict was found dead yesterday or it just wasn't front-page news.

On my way back across the parking lot to my truck I thought about Evan Walsh and his trip across the *Subway* parking lot. *Maybe I'll drive over there later today and have a look around,*

I was gone about twenty-five minutes, and when I got back to my apartment Angel was gone. The change and five dollar bill I had tossed on the coffee table before I lay down on the couch early in the morning was also gone. I wondered if anything else was missing. I wondered when I would see her again. I locked the front door and took a shower.

Chapter Seven

Later that morning I took Indian River Drive into work—a slower drive, but much more scenic. The swaying palm trees lulled me into believing I'd been transported into one of those classic Florida postcards; I half expected to see WELCOME TO THE SUNSHINE STATE written in cartoon letters across the impossibly blue sky. I wanted to have a look around the parking lot where Evan Walsh was stabbed. I decided to wear a dress shirt and sport coat and even stuck my gold shield in the inside breast pocket. I wouldn't come right out and say I was still a cop, but if someone assumed it, so be it. I didn't bring my weapon and I was wearing jeans and sneakers; no need to get too carried away. I was wearing my Ray-Ban Clubmasters however. I always felt they made me look more cop-ly.

I hung a left onto Orange Avenue and a quick right into the parking lot. I parked at the far end and walked back to the spot where Walsh had lain helpless on the ground. The two quarts of dried blood that still stained the blacktop almost seven weeks later marked the spot nicely. I adjusted my shirt as I walked. Either I'd shrunk it the last time I washed it, or I had put on a few pounds.

I hadn't thought about it when Spence described the crime scene, but the parking lot was situated at the *rear* of the businesses on Second Street. There was the Subway—where Walsh had purchased a sandwich. Subway sat nestled between a 7-Eleven—on the left—and a hair salon. Further down was a bistro, some offices, and a vacant store.

I stood over the blood spot with my hands on my hips. I stared at the stain for a while, then I glanced over at the back of Subway. It was too bright outside to see in through the window. If the clerk saw Walsh lying here, he must have looked out the back door. I scanned the parking lot wondering where Walsh was parked at the time. That's when I decided I had better call Tommy Franklin later. Maybe he would give me copies of the crime scene photos and the clerk's statement. Maybe even let me have a look at the security footage. I could just tell him the victim's family had asked me to look into it. They hadn't though. Maybe I should give Walsh's widow a call first, just to let her know what I was up to.

I walked the entire parking lot from Orange Avenue to Avenue A, and then around to Second Street. As I strolled along I surveyed the tops of every building in the area, looking for security cameras. I moved down Second Street and walked around the corner onto Orange Avenue, and then Indian River Drive. Halfway down Indian River I paused and removed my sunglasses. I rubbed my eyes and then wiped the sweat from my forehead with the sleeve of my sport coat. It was hot, and I wondered how I used to stand wearing a jacket to work every day. I felt a stream of sweat run down my ribcage.

East of the parking lot—on the other side of Indian River Drive—was the Fort Pierce Library, Gazebo Park, and a parking lot. Beyond that was Melody Lane and the marina.

I turned, walked back across the parking lot, and went into Subway through the back door. The place had opened for business an hour earlier and lunch was in full swing.

I walked up to the counter and a guy in line threw a thumb over his shoulder and said, "Line's back here pal." I ignored him, and pulled out my badge.

"Excuse me," I said to the oldest-looking of the three young men behind the counter. "I was wondering if I could ask you a few questions."

He glanced at the badge and nodded. "Let me just finish this sub," he said.

I walked back to the rear entrance and stared out at the parking lot. I had a clear view of the blood stain. I looked to my left at the men's room door.

The kid I spoke to at the counter squeezed past me and walked outside. I followed him. He pulled a pack of Marlboro Lights out of his shirt pocket and a lighter out of his pants pocket. He leaned against the railing at the top of the steps that lead to the parking lot below.

"Listen, man," the kid said. "My buddy admitted the weed was his. They told me the charges were dropped." He lit a cigarette and took a long drag.

The kid's name tag read JIMMY. "This isn't about weed, Jimmy, it's about the guy that was stabbed in the parking lot last month. I'm doing a follow-up investigation."

Jimmy breathed a sigh of relief. "Oh, Thank God."

"Yeah, thank God. Were you working that night, Jimmy?"

"What night?"

The future leaders of our world. Just speaking to kids that age gave me a headache. "The night the guy was stabbed."

Jimmy took another hit off the cigarette and smoke escaped from his mouth and nose as he spoke. "Oh. No, I wasn't here. I worked that night, but I got out at nine."

"Who *was* working that night?"

"It was Freddie."

"Freddie got a last name?" I reached inside my jacket for my notepad that hadn't been there in over three years. *Dammit.*

"His last name is Underwood." The kid's face lit up; I could tell he was experiencing a rare aha moment. "Wait a minute, if you're doing a follow-up investigation, shouldn't you already know his name?"

"Don't get smart kid. Just wanted you to corroborate the name on the police report."

"Sorry, sir."

"Forget it. The report said Freddie found the body." I was winging it. I hadn't seen a police report and had never heard the name Freddie Underwood before. "Said he came out of the men's room, looked out the door"—I motioned toward the door—"and saw the body in the parking lot." We both turned toward the bloodstain.

Jimmy shrugged his shoulders. "Yeah, I guess that's how it happened."

"You guess? Freddie never discussed it with you?"

"No. We were closed the next day—because of the murder—and Freddie had the next two days off. He came in the following day to pick up his check and told Craig—that's our manager—that he was quitting."

"Did you witness the conversation?"

"No. Craig told us about it later. He said Freddie was pretty shook up about finding that guy like that, and didn't feel safe working nights anymore."

"You got an address for Freddie?"

"Craig's not here till five."

"I'm not asking Craig, Jimmy. I'm asking you."

"Ummm," Jimmy stalled. "I don't know if—"

"Would you rather discuss the marijuana incident you *thought* I was here about?"

"I'll grab you that address," Jimmy said. "Give me a second." He took another long drag and flicked the cigarette into the parking lot.

I watched from the steps as Jimmy lumbered down the hall and around the corner. When he returned he was holding a piece of paper he had torn from a spiral notebook. "Here's Freddie's address, and his cell phone number too."

"Thanks, Jimmy." I shoved the paper into my pocket.

"You got a last name, Jimmy?"

"Yeah. Bertran. Why?"

"Just asking."

"Hey, don't tell Freddie I gave you his number. He's kind of a dick."

"Sure thing, Jimmy. And if you think of anything else that might be helpful"—I reached for my business cards that also hadn't been there in over three years. *Dammit!*—"give me a call."

Jimmy reached out his hand to take the business card that wasn't coming.

"I'll just call *you*," I said. I pulled the paper he had given me back out of my pocket. "Here, right your number on this."

Jimmy did as he was told. "You should get yourself a little notepad, dude."

"That's a good idea, Jimmy. I just might do that."

Jimmy grinned proudly. He knew he had come up with a great idea. Later he would probably post on Facebook about his idea for police officers to carry notepads. I wondered how many likes he would get. I wondered if a selfie would accompany his post. I wondered if Jimmy had eaten a lot of paint chips when he was a toddler.

I had removed my jacket, untucked my shirt, and rolled up my sleeves before I even got back to my truck. I was glad I didn't have to dress like that anymore. I brought a T-shirt, cargo shorts, and flip-flops with me. I would change when I got to the bar.

Chapter Eight

I walked into the bar with my sport coat draped over my arm. Allison was already behind the bar.

"You coming from church?" Melvin asked.

"Yeah," I responded. "I was praying for your sorry old soul."

Melvin laughed. I didn't stick around to see if he survived. Instead, I went on through the bar, down the hallway past the restrooms, and to my office. I tossed the jacket on the back of my chair and sat down behind the desk. I pulled the piece of paper from my pocket and tossed it on the desk next to the phone. Retrieving the phone book from a side drawer, and looking up Even Walsh's phone number, I called his widow.

"June?" I said when she answered. I hadn't spoken with June in at least six years—not since a hug, a kiss on the cheek, and a *sorry for your loss* at Evan's funeral.

"Yes?" she replied.

"It's Cole."

"Cole?"

"Cole Ballinger."

"Oh, of course … Cole. How are you?"

"Good, June. How are you?"

"I'm doing much better." There was a few seconds of silence and then June asked, "Is there something I can do for you, Cole?"

How should I word this? It had been awhile since I had spoken with a victim's next of kin. "Oh, yeah … I stopped by the Subway … where Evan was attacked." I waited. June didn't say anything so I continued. "I spoke with one of the employees there. He gave me the phone number of the guy who was working that night—the guy who found Evan, and called 911. He said that—"

"I don't understand, Cole," June interrupted. "Why were you there? I thought you retired from the police department."

"I did retire. I was just looking into the case."

"You lost me, Cole. Why would you be looking into Evan's murder?"

"Lynn asked me to," I told her. "She said that you had mentioned to her that the investigation had stalled."

"I did mention it to her, but I didn't expect her to get *you* involved. I'm sure the detectives are doing everything they can."

"I'm sure they are, June, but Lynn asked and I figured it wouldn't hurt to have some fresh eyes on the case and ask a few questions here and there."

"I don't want you to go to any trouble, Cole," June said. "I'm sure you have more than enough to keep yourself busy with the bar and all."

"The bar practically runs itself and I don't mind at all. The reason I called was to let you know that I was going to speak with the kid who was working that night and also give the lead detective on the case a call."

"Okay, I guess."

"Also, I was wondering if I could stop by sometime tomorrow afternoon and ask *you* a few questions."

"Ask *me* a few questions? What did you need to ask *me*?"

"I'd rather stop over, if that's okay. Is tomorrow good?"

"Actually, I'm leaving in a few hours and heading down to my sisters in West Palm. I won't be back until late Thursday evening."

"Can I stop by Friday evening?"

"Yes, I guess that would be fine. I'll see you then," she said, and hung up the phone.

I dialed Freddie Underwood's number and got his voicemail. I decided not to leave a message. Maybe I would just stop by his place unannounced. Although, he might not like that. I heard he was kind of a dick.

When I walked back out to the bar Melvin was still working on his first Scotch. He slowly spun his glass with his fingertips as he stared out the window behind the bar.

There were three other customers seated at the bar as well—a couple in their mid-twenties and a guy in his late fifties. The young couple were in beach attire; he had on swim trunks and a tank top, and she was wearing a bikini top with denim shorts.

The guy in his fifties was dressed in wannabe biker garb—a cop-lawyer-doctor suffering from a midlife crisis and playing macho dress-up in a zippered motorcycle jacket and leather pants—and looked a lot like James Brolin did twenty years ago. A German-style helmet sat in front of him on the bar. I'm sure the clueless clown thought he looked cool in it.

The young couple sat with their chairs turned toward each other and stared into each other's eyes as they spoke. Their bare knees were touching and they held hands. They were probably soul mates and best friends. I wanted to slap the kid upside the head and tell him what lies down the road, but he wouldn't listen. He probably tells his friends she's like no other girl he has ever met. The happy idiot.

The James Brolin-looking biker dude was in a conversation with my little girl, and she was hanging on his every word. She had the same look in her eye as Marcia Brady had when she opened the door to find Davy Jones standing there in all his adorable glory. A good-looking older man and an impressionable young girl is a lethal combination, so I did what any dad would do. I walked behind the bar, kissed her on the cheek, and said, "Run back in the kitchen and see if Leon needs any help."

"Norma's back there," Allison argued.

"And in a few seconds you'll be back there too."

Allison rolled her eyes. She probably didn't realize I was just trying to save that poor bastard's life.

Allison smiled at Brolin and said, "I'll talk to you later."

No you won't, I thought.

Brolin just nodded. He wasn't stupid. He didn't even turn and watch her butt as she walked to the kitchen. He wanted to. But I'm guessing he didn't want me to remove his eyes from his skull.

"How ya doing down there, Melvin?" I asked.

He raised his glass. "Halfway there," he said.

Allison was walking back toward the bar. "Leon said he didn't need me back there," she reported.

I pointed toward the kitchen. She rolled her eyes, spun around, and went back through the door.

"You kids need another?" I asked the young couple.

They both slid their empty Mic Ultra bottles across the bar. I reached into the cooler behind me and grabbed two more, being ever so careful not to grab a regular Michelob on accident. These two were probably headed to the gym afterwards to check in and take selfies in a mirror. One carb too many and they'd be the laughing stock of social media. I couldn't have that hanging over my head.

"How 'bout you?" I asked Brolin.

"No, thanks. I'm good. Gonna head out in a minute."

Good idea, I thought.

Norma stuck her head through the kitchen door and I waved her over. She jumped behind the bar and I went to the kitchen.

"Hey," I said.

"What?" Allison asked. Leon had her making side salads for dinner and wrapping the bowls in plastic wrap.

"You know a kid by the name of Jimmy Bertran? He's about your age and works over at the Subway on Second Street."

She shook her head. "Never heard of him. Why, did he say something about me?"

"Believe it or not, Allison, this isn't about you. Weird, huh?"

"Dad, I don't think *everything* is about *me*."

"How about a kid by the name of Freddie Underwood?"

"Yeah, I know him … well, I mean I don't know him, but I know *of* him. He's a few years older than me."

"How do you know *of* him?" I asked.

"Remember a few years ago when that abandoned house over on Havana Avenue burned down and that old homeless man died?"

"Yeah, I remember."

"It was Freddie Underwood who started the fire."

"That was him? I remember that fire. He got off because the cop who searched him didn't read him his rights or something."

"Right. I've heard other people say he brags about it sometimes when he gets drunk or stoned. He even told someone that he knew the old guy was in there and poured gas on him before he lit the fire."

"Jesus Christ." I guess he is a dick. "Why'd you keep quiet about this all this time?"

Allison chewed her lip. "I guess … I guess I just didn't want to get involved."

"Yeah. Too many people like that."

I shot her my patented disappointed dad look and walked over and peeked through the kitchen door.

"Hey," I said. "Why don't you jump back behind the bar and let Norma go back to whatever it was she was doing."

Allison grinned. "Why, is he gone?" she asked.

I played stupid. "Is who gone?"

"That guy at the bar you didn't want me talking to."

"Everything's not about you, Allison," I said, and walked out of the kitchen.

Chapter Nine

Between the lunch and dinner rush, when things quieted down, I walked out to one of the picnic tables and called Tommy Franklin.

"Hey, Tommy," I said when he answered the phone. "It's Cole Ballinger."

"Cole Ballinger. That's the second time in the last week I've heard your name. I also hear you're playing private cop now."

I laughed. "Not really. Just looking into the Evan Walsh case for an old friend."

"His wife, I assume."

"Actually for my ex."

"Your ex? Why would your ex be asking you to look into a murder investigation?"

"I guess to score points and rekindle an old friendship."

"Murder investigations: bringing people together," Franklin joked. "So, what can I do for you?"

"The kid who called it in, Freddie Underwood, I understand he was arrested a few years back for arson."

"Yeah that's right. The charges were dropped a few days later."

"There was a death in the fire, wasn't there?"

"Uh, yeah. A transient. I guess the guy broke in and was sleeping there nights. I doubt the kid even knew the old man was in there."

"He's been overheard bragging about pouring gas on the guy and lighting him on fire."

"Probably just trying to build up his street cred with his friends. Wants people to think he's a tough guy. You know how kids are these days."

"I guess. Has Underwood been picked up on anything since the arson?"

"Nope. Clean sheet after that."

"He ever say why he set the fire?"

"He never *said* a word. The kid lawyered up immediately and then the charges were dropped a few days later."

"Was Underwood ever considered a suspect in the Walsh stabbing?"

"No. Surveillance cameras inside the sub shop and the 911 time stamp confirmed his story. He wouldn't have had time to do it. Besides, he had no motive. He didn't even know Evan Walsh.

"You hear he quit his job a few days after the incident?"

"No, I didn't. But from what I can tell he bounces around from job to job anyway. If I remember correctly he had only been at Subway for a few weeks before the stabbing."

"I got Underwood's address and phone number from a co-worker. I may head over to his place later today and ask him a few questions, if you don't mind me sticking my nose in."

"Hey, feel free. If you find out anything you think I don't already know, give me a holler back."

"You got it, Tommy. It was nice talking to you."

"You too, Cole. Hey, how's that bar of yours doing? I've been meaning to stop in there some night after work."

"It's going good. You *should* stop in."

"I'll do that. Talk to you later." Franklin hung up the phone. The call went better than I thought it would. Usually cops don't like civilians poking around in their cases, and technically, I was a civilian now.

I kicked my flip-flops off and walked out to the beach. I removed my T-shirt and dropped it into the sand and then tossed my cell phone on top of the shirt. I walked between the scatterings of sunbathers and waded out into the warm ocean water up to my knee caps, and then dove in. Holding my breath as long as I could I swam out, staying below the surface as far as I could, and then came up for air. I floated on my back, watching the clouds move slowly across the sky above me. A seagull flew over. I always assume they are going to shit on me. This one didn't. Maybe I should play the lottery today.

I turned and swam back toward the shore. When I could touch the bottom, I stood and walked toward shore. Allison was waiting for me, standing ankle-deep in the water. She was holding two bottles of Bud Light. She handed one to me.

"Thanks," I said.

We both walked about three or four feet onto the shore, turned, and sat in the sand facing the water.

"So, what happened yesterday … with Angel?" Allison asked.

"Me and Kelly picked her up at some lowlife's house and I took her back to my place."

"She spend the night?'

"Yes."

"How did she look?"

"Good," I lied.

Allison knew I was lying. Angel hadn't looked *good* in years.

"She still at your place?"

"No, she left around eleven this morning."

"Where did she go?"

"I don't know."

Allison took a deep breath and then let out a long sigh. "I wish she would get her act together."

"Me too. What did you tell your mother?"

"I didn't tell her anything. She would have just asked me a million questions I didn't know the answers to. Then she would have called you and started a fight with you. Why say anything?"

I put my arm around Allison and kissed her on the temple. "I love you, princess."

"I love you too, Dad," she said.

We sat together in the sand staring out over the water until we finished our beers, and then we went back to work.

Chapter Ten

Tuesday night got a little busier than most Tuesday nights, so I never got a chance to speak with Freddie Underwood. I tried calling him one more time but once again got his voicemail. I decided to drive over to his place the following morning around eleven-thirty.

Freddie Underwood lived in the Tanglewood Trailer Park, about a mile down the road from my old house, on Weatherbee Road. I had driven by that trailer park almost every day for about six years on my way to and from work, but I think this was the first time I had gone in.

I drove slowly through the park reading each house number and finally located Freddie's trailer in the southwest corner of the park. I didn't know if Freddie lived alone or with roommates. For all I knew he still lived with his parents.

At the end of his street was a turnaround. I drove my truck around the circle and parked facing the way I had come in. From the looks of Freddie's trailer he could definitely afford the rent all on his own. It was a doublewide crafted in what I facetiously called the Early Tornado-Bait Style—sagging on cement blocks with a humongous TV antenna looming overhead and busted lattice covering up the undercarriage. I didn't know what color the trailer was in the mid-seventies when it was built, but in the last ten years some proud homeowner had painted it robin's egg blue. There was a ten-by-twelve deck attached to the side of the trailer and painted barn-red with steps that led down to the dirt driveway. There were no cars in the driveway but I didn't even know if Freddie owned a car.

I climbed out of my truck, walked up the driveway, and onto the deck. I pounded on the door with my fist and then wiggled the doorknob; it was locked. I walked to the end of the deck and looked around. To the east of Freddie's place was another trailer—it was newer and in much better shape—and to the west his deck over looked a vacant lot that sat on Route 1. I walked back to the door and knocked again. *Probably out setting homeless people on fire*, I thought, and then knocked one last time.

When it became obvious that Freddie wasn't home I put my face up to the window to the left of the front door and shaded my eyes from the light. It quickly became obvious that Freddie *was* home, but he wouldn't be answering the door. The young arsonist was lying face down in the middle of his living room floor in a pool of dried blood. I could tell from his caved-in skull that there was no reason to administer CPR.

All the windows in the trailer were jalousie windows—not great for climbing through. I checked the front door, and then walked around the trailer inspecting each window and then the backdoor. There was no sign of forced entry; Freddie probably knew his attacker.

I returned to my truck and grabbed a screwdriver that was in a little road-side assistance kit one of the kids had gotten me for Christmas a few years back. I wedged the screwdriver's flat blade in between the lockset and the doorjamb and popped open the front door with ease. The screwdriver left a dent in the soft metal of the jamb and the side of the door. I shoved the tool into my back pocket, went inside, and shut the door behind me.

The fifty-two inch high definition television was on but the sound was turned all the way down. *The Price Is Right* was on. I couldn't read lips so I had no idea what Drew Carey was saying—probably something about Rice-A-Roni in the Check-Out game. The TV looked brand new and just didn't fit with the rest of the décor; neither did the new Blu-ray player or the new Xbox. Seven or eight video game cases littered the top of the entertainment stand.

Freddie Underwood was wearing a red T-shirt with the sleeves cut off and a pair of blue and yellow board shorts. There was massive head trauma; it looked as though most of his blood and gray matter had gushed out of the hole in the back of his head seconds before he died. Once, when I was a uniformed cop, I had the misfortune of seeing what an aluminum bat can do to the back of someone's skull, and this looked very similar.

There was blood spatter on the TV screen and the wall behind the TV. I scanned the room for the bat or whatever the weapon may have been. I didn't see anything. At the south end of the trailer was an eat-in kitchen and at the north end, a hallway that led to two bedrooms and a bath. I didn't see a litter box or cat anywhere, so maybe Freddie didn't have one, but judging by the strong ammonia smell, someone at some time did. I nudged Freddie's thigh with the toe of my sneaker; stiff as a board.

On a plate on the kitchen table was a ham sandwich on white bread and an unopened can of Busch beer. Whoever killed poor Freddie wasn't expected for lunch. I poked the bread with my fingertip. It was just as stale as Freddie. The microwave still had the Energy Guide sticker stuck to the door. Either Freddie had recently appeared on The Price is Right, or he had come into some ill-gotten money. I doubted Subway had that great of a severance package.

I opened drawers and a few cabinet doors. I read notes and things that were pinned to a bulletin board and looked at photographs that were stuck to the refrigerator door with magnets. In a drawer next to the fridge I found the receipt for the microwave and Xbox and another receipt for the television. I checked the date stamp on each and then shoved them into my pocket. Should I have? No, but things were starting to add up and I was starting to feel like a cop again.

In an end table I found another receipt, this one was for the DVD player, some DVDs, and a few video games. I kept that one too. All told, Freddie had spent about $2700 between May 2 and May 25. I grabbed a dry washcloth from the bathroom and wiped down anything I had touched. On my way out I pulled the door shut holding the knob with the washcloth and then shoved it into my pocket with the receipts.

I figured Tommy Franklin would be put on the Freddie Underwood murder case because Freddie was at the scene of Walsh's murder. I also knew I had pretty much sabotaged his investigation. When Franklin got to Freddie's trailer, he would see signs of forced entry, thanks to my screwdriver. He also wouldn't find the receipts showing Freddie had spent a bunch of cash in the days following Evan Walsh's murder. Oh well, what are ya gonna do?

Chapter Eleven

When I left Freddie's place I made a right onto Weatherbee Road and a right at the next corner, and then a right onto White City Road. When I got to the next corner I waited at the red light. From where I sat I could see past the CVS—which sat at the corner of White City Road and Route 1—into the Liquor World parking lot. The old brown Plymouth Duster was once again sitting right out front.

The light turned green and I crossed the highway and turned right into the Winn-Dixie parking lot. Drove around behind CVS and into the parking lot that was shared by Liquor World, Enterprise Rent-A-Car, and a couple other businesses. I parked in a space near Route 1 and shut off the engine.

There was no one in the Duster, and I couldn't see inside the liquor store from where I sat. I wondered if Angel was with them. I waited about ten minutes and then out walked the nasty bastard I had throat-punched two days earlier; he was alone. Maybe he would make it through the day without getting throat-punched again. He started the piece of shit, backed out of his spot, and headed down
Route 1.

I jumped out of my truck and went inside the liquor store. I glanced down at my T-shirt, shorts, and flip-flops and wished I was dressed more like a cop. Other than me and the clerk, the store was empty.

The clerk had his back to me and was straightening bottles of booze that sat on a shelf behind the counter. He was completely bald on top but the hair on the sides and back of his head was pulled back into a greasy foot-long ponytail. The back of his white T-shirt was soaked through with sweat making it almost transparent. He needed his back shaved.

"Excuse me," I said.

He turned. "Yeah?"

"The guy who just left, the guy driving that old Plymouth Duster."

The clerk leaned forward placing the palms of his hands on the counter. His palms were massive but his fingers were no larger than Vienna sausages. "What about him?"

"You know him?"

"Yeah, I know him. Why?"

"Can you give me his name?"

"I could, but I won't. I don't know you, man."

I glanced up at the security camera that was pointing right at me. I guessed I wouldn't be throat-punching *this* fat prick. "Listen, I was coming out of the car rental place next door and I saw him back into my truck just before he pulled away. I figured if I could get his name, we could handle it just between the two of us. You know, not getting any cops or insurance companies involved."

He stared at me for a second. "Show me," he said.

"Show you?"

"The damage to your vehicle. If there's damage I'll give him a call and give *him your* number."

I shrugged. "Okay. Follow me."

The two of us walked—he waddled—across the parking lot toward my truck with me leading the way. As we neared the side of the truck I pointed at an area above the driver's side rear wheel. "Right there. See the dent?"

When he leaned in for a closer look I grabbed the back of his head and slammed it into the fender. He dropped to his knees, and at the same time I shoved him back against the truck, grabbing his index and middle fingers and bending them back as far as I could without snapping them.

"Listen, you fat piece of shit. I'm going to ask you one more time what that scumbag's name is and where he lives. And if you don't tell me, I'll rip off these two fingers and shove them so far up your ass you'll be able to scrape that crusty shit off your teeth. You got it?"

He shook his head and tried to say yes, but it came out more like a pig's squeal. He gave me the name—Ted

Hale—and address I was looking for. *Still no note pad in my pocket.*

The tub of lard seemed grateful when I released my grip on his little sausage fingers, and he wouldn't notice the welt on the side of his head until he looked in a mirror. I wondered what the odds of him calling the police were. I guessed they were probably pretty slim, especially if he and Ted were involved in anything drug-related together, and they probably were.

I started my truck and rolled down the window. The four-hundred-pounder was doing his best to climb to his feet.

"Hey," I said.

"Yeah?" he groaned.

"Thanks for your help. If I need anything else, I'll be back."

"Whatever," he mumbled and waddled back to the liquor store.

Chapter Twelve

On my way to The Breakwater I phoned Spence Oller.

"Hey, Spence," I said.

"Hey, Cole," he answered.

"I was wondering if you could do me a little favor?"

"Sure," he replied eagerly.

"Can you run a check on a guy by the name of Ted Hale? His address is 6801 Oleander Avenue in White City. And let's just keep this one between the two of us."

"Yeah, I can do that as soon as I get back to the station. I'll run by the bar later this afternoon and let you know what I got."

"You can just call me back if you want. You don't have to go out of your way."

"That's okay, I don't mind." There was a pause. "Is Allison working today?"

"She's on from one till six today, Spence. Why do you ask?" I knew why he asked. Poor bastard didn't have a chance. He's too young and he looks nothing like James Brolin.

From the end of the Seaway Drive Bridge to The Breakwater Grill there were six new buildings going up; four of them were restaurants. I didn't know what the other two places were going to be, but it was a safe bet they'd be gift shops where tourists could buy two-dollar pieces of shit for twenty bucks each. I know that sounds like a huge markup for shit but each turd has "Florida" written on the side of it. That's a goddamn bargain, I don't care who you are.

Every parking spot in front of the bar was taken, so I drove around Jetty Park and pulled into a spot on the other side of the park facing the bar. Oh, well, I could use a walk through the palm trees. Who couldn't? I hoped the lack of parking spots indicated a busy day for the bar. I could also use a busy day. I wondered how many busy days there would be after the four new restaurants opened up.

"Hi, Daddy," Allison said the second I walked through the door.

"Hi, baby," I responded. "No Melvin today?"

"Not so far."

"Been busy?"

"Busier than usual."

There were eight people at the bar. *Nice!*

I leaned my elbow on the end of the bar and nodded to the guy closest to me. "How's it going?"

"Good," he replied.

I held up my hand with my thumb and finger about three inches apart. "Can you pour me a little ginger ale, Allison? No ice."

She paid no attention to my fingers but stopped texting long enough to fill the glass.

"Thanks," I said.

I glanced around the room at the customers. There was a small seating area in the same room as the bar; it only sat sixteen people—four tables of four. Through a doorway across from the bar was another larger dining room that held about forty diners. There were three people sitting at one of the tables in the bar and six others were seated at two tables in the larger room. I went to the door that faced the ocean. There were six more people seated at the picnic tables outside. Pretty good lunch crowd for a Wednesday.

I watched as Norma and two other servers—Emily Travis and Dalia Medina—darted briskly about the place clearing tables, taking orders, and delivering food. I walked back over with a smile on my face and leaned against the bar to finish my soda.

"Daddy, did you hear they're opening a TGI Friday's right down the street?" Allison asked. "I can't wait."

"Yeah, nether can I."

It was around three o'clock Wednesday afternoon that Spence wandered in carrying a few sheets of computer paper that were stapled together. He tried not to smile when he saw Allison behind the bar. I was also behind the bar restocking the beer cooler.

"Hi, Allison," he said as he loosened his tie and climbed onto one of the barstools.

"Hey, Spence," said Allison. "What can I get you?"

"Ginger ale. Thanks."

"I had no idea that ginger ale was a cop drink," Allison said as she grabbed the soda gun. "I mean I knew about donuts and coffee, but the ginger ale thing was something I just never knew."

Allison was joking of course, but Spence was never one to catch on really quick. He was a smart guy, maybe just smart enough to over-think the average joke.

Spence cocked his head like a Yorkie hearing the word treat. "Do a lot of cops order ginger ale?" he asked.

"No, I was—never mind."

I slammed the cooler door closed and tossed the empty card board case over the bar and onto the floor.

"How's it going, Spence?" I asked.

"Can't complain." Spence removed his sunglasses and laid them on the bar. Then he removed his cell phone from a clip attached to his belt and laid it on the bar next to the glasses. "Here you go," he said, pushing the papers across the bar to me. "Everything we got on one Mr. Ted Hale. Seems to be quite the low life piece of crap." He glanced over at Allison. "Excuse my French."

I didn't know crap was a French word. Le crap, *maybe*. I had known Spence for at least five years and crap was the first swear word I had ever heard him use. I guess hanging around a squad room full of cops was really corrupting the poor boy. I imagined he was on a dangerous downward spiral and would soon be drinking non-alcoholic beer and saying, "fart" and "darn it."

I picked up the paper and began reading. Spence was right: Ted Hale was a piece of crap.

Ted spent most of his early life in foster homes, getting adopted by the Hale family when he was eleven. The police had visited the Hale farm a number of times between 2004 and 2012, mostly for domestic complaints. Norman Hale died from a massive stroke in 2013. Carol Hale battled cancer for over ten years and died soon after Norman. Ted inherited the farm and still lived there. He sold all the livestock and machinery as he needed money and bounced around from one shitty job to another. He now worked at Liquor World on Route1. *Well, there's something Jabba the liquor salesman forgot to mention.*

When I finished reading the report I knew an awful lot about Ted Hale—a lot more than Angel probably knew about him.

I tossed the papers on the bar behind me. "Thanks, Spence. That was a very thorough report, to say the least. You got all that from police reports?"

"Well, I made a few calls and asked around."

"You were supposed to keep it between you and me."

"I didn't mention your name."

"Thanks, Spence. I owe you one."

Spence shot a look toward Allison at the end of the bar and then leaned in. "Fix me up with your daughter," he whispered.

"What!" I asked a little too loudly.

Allison spun around.

There was a fearful look in Spence's eye. He made a quick shushing noise. We all three stared at each other until Allison turned back around.

"I'm not setting her up with anyone, Spence," I told him. "I can't believe you would even ask something like that."

"Well, you said you owed me one."

"I didn't mean my firstborn."

"What is it you don't like about me, Cole?" Spence asked.

"I do like you, Spence."

"Then what's the problem? Is there someone else you would rather she dated? I have a good job, a nice home. I have money in the bank. I've never done drugs and I rarely drink alcohol. I'm good to my mother."

Spence's argument was a good one, but I couldn't let him know that. "Sorry, Spence, I'm not passing my little girl a note that says 'Do you like Spence? Check yes or no.'"

"She's not a little girl."

Our voices were growing a bit louder. "She will always be *my* little girl and you can't have her."

Allison turned around again. "It's not up to you to decide who *gets* me and who *doesn't.* I'm an adult and I'll date whomever I please."

Neither Spence nor I said a word; we just stared.

Allison continued. "I'm twenty-two years old, I'll be twenty-three in a month, and I decide who I date." She turned her attention to Spence. "Spence, I would love to go out with you. Just let me know when and where."

I threw up my hands. "Well, that's just great. I guess I have nothing to say about this." I stormed out from behind the bar, went into my office, and slammed the door behind me. I waited in silence for about fifteen seconds and then pumped my fist. *Yes!* I thought. *Spence is going to make a great son-in-law.* That little plan worked perfectly.

Chapter Thirteen

On Friday morning I was on my way to the bar when I got a call from Tommy Franklin.

"What's up, Tommy?" I answered.

"Cole, you ever get a chance to speak with Freddie Underwood?"

"Not yet, Tommy. It's been pretty busy at the bar and I just haven't had a chance. I'm supposed to see the victim's wife tonight, though. Maybe I'll get over there and speak to Underwood tomorrow some time."

"I'm afraid that won't be possible, Cole."

"Oh yeah, why's that?"

"The manager of the trailer park where he lives found him this morning. He was lying on the floor of his trailer. Someone bashed his brains in."

"That sucks. You think it's a coincidence that the kid who found Walsh is now dead?"

"Who knows? I'm at the trailer now waiting for Crime Scene to finish up."

"You mind if I stop over there, Tommy?"

"If you want to."

"I'll be there in ten minutes." I hung up and made a U-turn on Route 1 and headed south. I figured if I got a good look around the crime scene I wouldn't slip up later and say something I wasn't supposed to know. Also, if a finger print of mine was found in his trailer, there would be a reason. Sure, I would be getting there after Crime Scene finished, but it would just look like someone made a mistake.

I took a left off of Weatherbee into the trailer park and followed the same path I had taken before. When I got to the turnaround at the end of Freddie's street, I entered it, turned around, and parked in the same spot I had parked a few days earlier. If anyone questioned a witness in a few days, they wouldn't remember if they saw my truck there the day of the murder, or two days after.

There was an ambulance, a county coroner's vehicle, and several marked and unmarked cars at the scene. Uniforms were canvassing the area and knocking on doors. Hopefully none of the park residents had even noticed the red Ford F-150 on Wednesday morning.

An officer I didn't recognize stopped me at the foot of the steps. "Sorry, pal, it's a crime scene."

Tommy spotted me through the window and hollered "He's alright. Let him in."

"Go ahead, pal," the uniform said.

The first thing I noticed when I entered Freddie's trailer was that Freddie smelled a lot worse on Friday than he did on Wednesday. We could thank the Florida heat for that one.

Tommy pulled back the sheet that was draped over Freddie. There were maggots feeding off his rotting brain. "You recognize him?" Tommy asked.

I put my hand over my mouth. "Jesus Christ, Tommy!"

Tommy laughed and dropped the sheet. "No one ever finds the body before it starts to stink."

"*Someone* knew the body was here." I walked around the trailer just as I had done before. "Crime Scene finish up?" I asked.

"Pretty much," Tommy answered.

"You mind if I look around?"

"Help yourself."

I made sure to look at everything I had already looked at and open every door and drawer I had previously opened. I didn't find anything new. I sure didn't find any receipts.

"You said this kid bounced around from job to job?" I asked.

"Yeah, I don't think he ever kept a job for more than a few months."

I pointed at the entertainment stand. "New TV, new X-box, and a new DVD player," I said.

"Yeah," Tommy said. "Got a new microwave in the kitchen as well."

"You don't say. Looks like Freddie must have come into some money recently."

"His landlord said he was three months behind in rent awhile back but he paid it up to date about three weeks ago."

"How much is the rent on a shit hole like this?"

"Five-fifty a month."

"So we're looking at about two grand plus the TV and the other new stuff."

"Looks that way."

"So who paid Freddie Underwood four thousand dollars to kill Evan Walsh?"

"The coroner's report said there were two attackers."

"Two huh?" Spence had already told me there were two assailants but I pretended I was hearing it for the first time. "I wonder if they each got four grand?"

"Or maybe the second attacker was the one who paid Underwood. Maybe he didn't want to do it alone."

"Or she," I remarked. "Freddie got a girlfriend?"

"Not that I'm aware of. Even if he did, why would his girlfriend want Walsh dead?"

I shrugged my shoulders. "Who knows? Just throwing it out there. None of the neighbors saw anything?"

"I have some guys going door to door, but I haven't heard anything yet."

"I guess the neighborhood watch wasn't doing its job."

"Didn't you used to live around here somewhere?"

"About a mile up the road."

"Your ex still have the place?

"Yup." I scanned the room one more time. "Other than Freddie's shopping spree, nothing else here seems to be out of the ordinary."

I did what I had come there to do—put myself in the trailer—and I was ready to leave. Freddie's stench was messing with my sinuses. There were places I would much rather be. For example: standing behind my bar and serving drinks to sunburnt tourists in skimpy bikinis.

I shook Tommy's hand. "Thanks for including me in this," I said.

"No problem," Tommy replied. "You said you were speaking with the widow this evening?"

"Yeah. I'll probably head over there after dinner."

I turned toward the door and Tommy slapped me on the back. "It was good seeing you, Cole. Stay out of trouble."

"I'll try my best, Tommy. I'll try my best."

Chapter Fourteen

I spent most of Friday afternoon staring at the clock on the wall across from the bar. Usually I enjoyed being at the bar; it was a relaxing place to be. But if I wasn't thinking about Angel and Ted Hale, I was thinking about Freddie Underwood and whatever scumbag gave him four thousand dollars to kill Evan Walsh. I tried to think back to when I was a cop and wondered if I ever relaxed at all during those twenty-five years. Maybe I had just been away from it for too long.

Melvin was at the bar sipping his Scotch and lemon, and around three Kelly Morgan walked through the door.

"Thank God it's Friday," Kelly said.

"You got that right," Melvin agreed.

"Every day is Friday for you," I told Melvin.

"Up yours," was Melvin's reply.

85

Kelly jumped up on a bar stool. "Bud Light Lime," he ordered, and then turned to Melvin. "You worked for the railroad, didn't ya, Melvin?"

"Forty years," said Melvin.

"What year did you retire?"

"Well, let's see," Melvin said, looking up at the ceiling as though the answer was written there. "Started in 1951 and retired in 1991."

"Jeeze," Kelly said. "I was only twelve years old when you retired."

"How the hell old are you?" Melvin asked.

"Thirty-eight."

"Are ya shittin' me? I thought you were as old as Cole."

I laughed out loud.

"Thanks, Melvin," Kelly said. He grabbed the neck of his beer and downed half the bottle in the first swig. "Ahh. I needed that."

Kelly was thirty-eight and had a great job. He owned a nice home, with a fairly new truck and a brand new Harley in the garage. Kelly was also single and had never been married. Kelly was the smartest man I knew.

Norma jumped behind the bar, so me and Kelly headed out to one of the picnic tables to drink our beers and chat. We would have invited Melvin to come along but he was one of the reasons we walked outside. We sat side by side on the same bench, facing the water, with our backs against the table, like we usually did.

"So, how did everything go with Angel the other day?" Kelly asked.

"As expected," I said. "She slept until almost noon the next day and when I ran to the store she stole six bucks and bolted. Thanks for getting my truck back to my place though."

"No problem. You see her since Tuesday?"

"No, but I've seen the douche she's hanging around with. His car was at the same liquor store on Wednesday. I got a name, Ted Hale, and an address on him. Turns out he works at that liquor store."

"It's like being a cop again," Kelly pointed out.

"You have no idea." I started to tell Kelly about Freddie Underwood and the murder of Evan Walsh, but he didn't know any of those people; he had never even met my ex before. I would have had to explain to him who everyone in the story was, so I just kept my mouth shut about it.

"Angel ever been in rehab?" he asked.

"Three times," I said. "The first time she finished a ninety-day program. She swore she would never do drugs again—said she couldn't believe what she had done to herself. She started going to school again and was doing really well. That lasted two months. The second time she left the facility after three days, and the third time she stayed for a whole week."

"That sucks. How old is she?"

"Nineteen."

Kelly just shook his head. "You got the guy's name, address, and you know where he works. What are you gonna do with that information?"

"Who knows?

Norma stuck her head through the door. "You guys need another beer?" she hollered.

"That would be great," I called back. *I should have married Norma,* I thought. Norma brought me beer whenever I needed one. Norma brought me food whenever I was hungry. Norma never bitched at me about stupid things. I never had to hear about Norma's tough day. Norma did anything I asked her to do, without question. Sure, I had to pay Norma to do those things for me, but hey, I was still paying Lynn and she didn't do any of those things—never did, really. If I knew then what I know now, I would have hired a waitress instead of getting married. I always imagined Norma's husband was one lucky bastard, but then again, she's his wife, not his waitress. I wonder if he has to hear about her tough day every night over dinner. She probably bitches about the asshole she has to bring beers to, bring plates of food to, and all the stupid shit she has to do without question.

"We could pay him a visit," Kelly said.

"Pay who a visit?" I asked.

"Ted Hale."

"Oh, right."

"Show up with baseball bats and break a leg or an arm. He might get the message."

"Sounds like a good plan, but somehow it would end with you and me sitting in a jail cell."

Norma returned with our beers and handed us each a bottle.

"Thanks, Norma," Kelly said. "Your Calvin is one lucky guy."

Norma shot him a look. "Try tellin' him that," she said. "Last week I found out he's been texting some thirty-year-old girl where he works. Found naked pictures on his phone ... of him and her. Sexting, the kids call it. He's fifty-nine years old. I've been scrubbin' shit stains out of his drawers for over thirty years and he's sending pictures of his dick to some little red-headed whore."

Norma went on for another ten or fifteen minutes while Kelly and I stared at the rapid movement of her jaw. About halfway through her tirade I had decided that I was glad I had never married Norma. When she was done she spun around and headed back toward the door.

"Yeah, that Calvin is one lucky son of a bitch," Kelly said.

Chapter Fifteen

Sometime after Lynn and I divorced, Evan and June Walsh had moved from their modest home on Boston Avenue into a much nicer home in the gated ocean-front community of Ocean Village. Situated along an executive par-3, nine-hole golf course, Ocean Village was made up of luxury homes and townhouses and was complete with its own restaurant, tiki bar, bank, and private beach.

I entered Ocean Village through the A1A entrance onto Clipper Boulevard, took a left at Windward Drive and drove the fifteen mile-per-hour speed limit to the end and around the corner onto Southstar Drive. The Walsh home sat at the corner of Southstar and Southpointe. I pulled into the driveway and shut off the engine.

So, this is how the other half live, I thought. I walked up to the front door and rang the bell.

June Walsh pulled the door open before the chimes quit ringing whatever tune that was. "Good evening,

Cole," she said. Fresh out of the shower, obviously, June was wearing a long white terry cloth robe. Her dark shoulder-length hair was wet and combed straight back and tight against her head.

I wondered if people had to stop saying hello and start saying good evening when they moved to Ocean Village. I figured they also had to start pronouncing "schedule" with the sh sound and saying "advertisement" like the Canadians and British, with the emphasis on *vert*. Why does having money make people talk weird? I wondered if one of the buildings I passed on my way in was a learning center to help rich people speak like assholes.

"Good evening," I replied. Saying good evening made me feel like Count Dracula. I wonder how wealthy Count Dracula was. I bet if he lived in Florida today he would live in Ocean Village.

At first glance it became obvious that saying good evening was not the only thing different about June. Her breasts were slightly larger, her nose was different, her lips were fuller, and I think her teeth were even whiter. She looked good, but in an odd way. Maybe someone who didn't know her before wouldn't notice, but I couldn't help thinking somebody had replaced the June Walsh I knew with a Stepford Wife.

"Won't you come in?" she asked.

Yes, I won't, I thought. I stepped through the door. June turned and walked into the living room. I shut the door behind me and followed her. I had to admit, June smelled really nice—no doubt from the coconut bath oil I forced myself not to picture her applying liberally to those store-bought titties.

"Please, have a seat." She waved her hand toward the couch like a spokesmodel at a boat show. "I just made coffee ... or would you rather have something stronger?"

"Coffee's good, thanks." I walked across the white carpeting to the sofa, hoping I hadn't stepped in dog shit on my way in. Then I remembered reading in the Ocean Village brochure that dog shit wasn't allowed inside the walls of their exclusive commune.

Almost everything in the Walsh house was either white or off-white, from moldings and ceilings, to walls, carpeting, and ceramic tile. I was very uncomfortable being there. I decided right then to never become wealthy.

June returned carrying a silver tray with two cups of coffee, a bowl of sugar cubes, and a small crystal pitcher of cream. She set it on the coffee table in front of me. "Help yourself," she said.

I picked up my cup, blew into it, and took a sip.

"So, what exactly brings you here, Cole?" June asked.

"I just wanted to feel like crap about my own pathetic lifestyle and social inferiority," I replied, and drank some more of her amazing coffee.

June smiled. "Cole, you were always so funny."

Really? I thought. People had called me a lot of things through the years but funny wasn't usually one of them. I just smiled back.

"I spoke with Detective Franklin on Tuesday right after I spoke with you. I told him I was looking into Evan's murder."

"Did you make sure to tell him it wasn't me who asked you to?"

"I told him it was Lynn who asked. I only called him to give him a heads up. I didn't want him to get pissed if he found out from someone else."

"What did he say?"

"He said he didn't mind. Then this morning he called me and told me that Freddie Underwood had been murdered." I waited for some kind of reaction from June but none came.

"Who's Freddie Underwood?" she asked.

"He was the kid who worked at Subway, the one who found Evan and called 911."

"Oh. Killed … how?"

"Someone attacked him at his trailer."

"A knife?"

"No, a baseball bat, or a pipe or something."

Her eyes drifted off toward the front. "My God, that's horrible."

"So, you never met Freddie?"

"Met him?" Her head turned back toward me. "Where would I have met him, Cole?"

"I'm just asking. I didn't know if maybe you and Evan had eaten at that Subway before. Maybe you knew him from there."

"We had never been there before. I don't even know why Evan was there. We always got our take-out from Lorenzo's, and he had already eaten dinner."

"What was Evan doing out that late the night he was attacked?" I asked.

"He had shown a house over on Avenue T. The guy he was showing it to worked until nine that evening so Evan said he would meet him at the property after work."

"You have that man's name?"

"I don't remember his name but I gave it to Detect Franklin. Do you think this man had something to do with Evan's murder?"

"I don't know."

"What about Freddie Underwood, you think *he* had something to do with it?"

"Hard to say, but it seems like quite a coincidence that he turned up dead a few weeks later."

"Maybe showing the house was a setup, a ruse to get Evan out of the house that evening," June suggested.

"Let's not get ahead of ourselves, June."

"You're right, Cole, I shouldn't let my imagination get the best of me."

"What about you and Evan?" I asked.

"What about us?"

"Was everything good between the two of you?"

"Good? What do you mean by good? We had our arguments, like most married couples, but things were fine, I guess."

"I remember the two of you went through a little rough patch around the time Lynn and I split up."

"Is there a question in there, Cole?"

"I guess not." I sipped my drink. "The two of you never had children."

Lynn smiled. "Is that a comment about our sex life?"

I shrugged.

"Are you sure you wouldn't like something stronger, Cole?" June asked. "I think I'm going to make myself a drink." When June stood the robe opened slightly and I got a quick glance as the muscle of her inner thigh flexed. Our eyes met and she grinned.

I could use a drink. "What do you have?"

"What would you like?" she asked.

"Scotch over ice?"

"Coming right up." June turned and left the room. I couldn't stop thinking about her legs. I watched her as she walked out of the room and hoped she wouldn't quickly turn around and catch me.

When June returned she was holding two rocks glasses; she handed mine to me. She had decided on Scotch as well. When she sat, I took a sip of my drink and made a conscious effort not to look at her legs or the cleavage that had now made a showing.

Wow! I thought. That's nothing like the Scotch I drink.

"How is it?" June asked.

"Very good." I breathed in the aroma before pulling the glass away from my nose.

"It's Macallan. Evan was saving it for a special occasion."

I'm sure I was supposed to be impressed but I had never heard of Macallan Scotch; and I own a bar. Just the posh way she said Macallan assured me that I would never be offering it at The Breakwater Grill. "Is this a special occasion?" I asked.

"Two old friends reconnecting. *I* would call that a special occasion."

I raised my glass. "To old friends," I toasted. I didn't have the heart to tell her we weren't friends.

After three more glasses of Scotch the conversation began to stray from her and Evan's relationship to what I had done with my life over the last thirteen years. On one trip to the den to refill our glasses June decided to go ahead and bring the bottle back to the living room with her. She set the bottle on the coffee table and took a seat beside me on the couch. She pulled her legs up underneath her revealing more bare skin.

Sometime during the conversation she caught me glancing down at the gap in her robe. The side of her right breast was exposed.

"I had them done a few years back," she said. "A birthday gift from Evan."

More like a birthday gift for *Evan*, I thought. I gave her a feigned look of confusion. "Done?" I asked.

She didn't buy it. She pulled open her robe to reveal Evan's purchase. They were a firm and perky C cup—the breasts of a twenty-year-old on a forty-eight-year-old woman. *Thank you, Evan.*

June leaned in and we kissed. The teenage boy inside my head thrust my hand inside the robe. I had never felt a fake breast in my life, but I wanted to. I'm here to tell you, it felt pretty damn good.

She pushed me back on the couch as she pulled open her robe, and climbed on top of me. *Happy early birthday to me.*

Chapter Sixteen

Sometime during the night we moved from the couch to the living room floor, and then to the bedroom.

My head was throbbing and I felt a little nauseous the second I opened my eyes; I wasn't used to drinking like that. June lay asleep next to me in bed, with only a sheet covering us. June's sheets were as smooth as her Scotch. I knew it had something to do with thread count, but when you buy your sheets at Walmart for eleven bucks, a high thread count is not usually what you're after.

June was on her stomach and I was on my back. I carefully pulled my arm out from underneath her so as not to wake her. As I did so, I wondered if we were now friends. She turned onto her side and I was free.

I hadn't spent the night with a woman in quite some time, especially a woman I knew. I wondered if there were any new rules or etiquette I wasn't aware of. I wouldn't mind if she got up and made me breakfast. I wondered if she was pretending to be asleep so she wouldn't have to, and I would just sneak out quietly. I guess my stomach wasn't really up for breakfast anyway.

I swung my legs over the side of the bed, got up, and went to the living room in search of my clothing. June's robe lay on the floor next to the couch. My shorts were next to it and I finally found my boxers jammed down in between the cushions.

I glanced at the grandfather clock in the hall on my way out the door, it was six-thirty. I wondered if I should have left a note.

By the time I got home, showered, and got dressed I was feeling a little better and wanted some breakfast. I checked the fridge; there were no eggs, bacon, or sausage. Not even a lousy Eggo, or one of those Jimmy Dean heart-attack-in-a-box breakfast sandwiches that I loved so much. I checked the cupboards; there were no Pop-Tarts or breakfast cereal. I couldn't remember the last time I had visited the grocery store. I knew Leon wasn't at work yet, so I couldn't ask him to make me breakfast. I wondered what he would do if I showed up at his house and asked him to make me something. That would probably be an excuse for *him* to get even and shoot *me*.

I wondered if Norma was up and making breakfast for her husband or if they were fighting about sexting or whatever form of social media he was using to pick up women.

I climbed in my truck and drove down to Mulligan's in Jensen Beach. I could get a great breakfast there, and an even better Bloody Mary. Did I need a Bloody Mary after the night before? No, but they make one you can't refuse. Hair of the dog and all.

I walked in and sat at a four top on the front dining room. I ordered my Bloody Mary when my waitress brought me a menu. "I'll be right back with that," she said. Her name tag said Karen.

"Thank you," I said, and smiled. I was smiling a little more than usual. I knew it was the sex.

I scanned the menu and decided on the breakfast burrito. I closed the menu and watched a boat dangle from a steel cable at a boat rental across the street.

When Karen returned with my drink she said, "There ya go," and then took my order.

I leaned back in my chair, and sipped my Bloody Mary. It was spicy, just the way I liked it. It was garnished with a huge green olive, a celery stalk, and a jumbo shrimp.

I stared at another waitress's butt across the room as she went from one table to the next. At one point she even dropped her pen and had to bend over and pick it up. I was really enjoying the show … until she turned around. "Hi, Mr. Ballinger," she said as she walked toward me.

Jesus Christ! It was one of Allison's friends from high school. Good God I'm old.

"Hi, Sherry," I replied. "I didn't know you were working here." My voice cracked a little when I spoke.

"I started last week. You come here often?"

"About once a month."

"How's Allison doing?"

"Good. She's working at the bar with me."

"Oh, that's nice. I don't think I could work all day with *my* dad."

"Sherry, can you give me a hand in here?" another waitress called out from the kitchen door.

"Sure," Sherry hollered back. "It was nice seeing you, Mr. Ballinger. Tell Allison I said hey."

"I will, Sherry."

As Sherry walked away from my table I turned my head in the opposite direction and stared across the street. I may be an old man, but I'm not a *perverted* old man.

Karen returned with my meal a few minutes later and it was as good as ever.

On my way out, I walked over to Sherry who was clearing a table near the door. "Sherry," I asked, "do you remember a kid from school named Freddie Underwood?"

"Yeah, I remember him," she said. "He was a little older than me and Allison."

"How about Jimmy Bertran?"

"I don't remember *him*. Did he go to school with us?"

"I'm not sure."

"Why, did they get arrested for something?"

"Why would you ask that?"

"Well, I remember Freddie used to get in trouble an awful lot. He burned down a building once, I think. And someone told me he killed an old man, or something. I never really believed it, though."

Looks like Freddie did indeed build up his street cred, I thought. "No, neither one of them was arrested. Their names just came up in a conversation the other day." I figured there was no need to tell Sherry about Freddie's death. I'm sure that's something young girls don't want to think about all day at work.

I told Sherry good bye for the second time, and as I turned toward the door I caught a glimpse of a slight smile. "What?" I asked.

"Nothing," she replied.

"Must be something."

"I just remembered this one time. Allison and I were sixteen, I think. We asked Freddie if he would buy beer for us; he was already twenty-one—"

"You and Allison?" I asked, just to make sure I had heard her right, and was now listening to a story about my sixteen-year-old daughter asking an arsonist and possible murderer to buy her beer.

"It was a long time ago," she blurted out, wondering if she had made a mistake in telling me the story. "It was the first time either one of us had drunk alcohol."

"It's okay," I assured her. "It's not like I can ground either one of you."

Sherry laughed. "Right?" she said, because for some reason kids now days have to say *right* in the form of a question whenever someone states the obvious.

"Go on," I told her.

"He bought our beer and then he said he wouldn't give it to us"—her voice dropped to an embarrassed whisper—"unless we let him touch our boobs."

Oh, this story just keeps on getting better. I groaned on the inside, not so sure I wanted to hear the rest of it. I didn't say anything, I didn't ask anything. I just stared at Sherry, hoping for a quick end to the tale.

"We let him touch them—over our shirts, of course."

"Of course," I said.

Sherry blushed a little. "He was such a dirtbag."

I left Mulligan's and climbed into my truck. As I drove along I thought about how well my morning was going—right up until the point where I had to hear about my daughter, only sweet sixteen, letting some scumbag molest her for a six-pack of beer. *Ugh!*

I drove North on Indian River Drive toward Fort Pierce. I wondered why Allison hadn't told me the story of Freddie buying her the beer when I asked her if she knew him. I was sure it hadn't slipped her mind. If she was embarrassed about the groping she could have left that part out.

My cell phone vibrated in my pocket. I pulled it out and looked at the number on the screen. It looked familiar to me, so I answered.

"Hello?" I said.

"Cole?" a woman asked.

"Yes."

"It's June."

"Oh, hey, June … sorry about sneaking out this morning."

She laughed. "You don't have to apologize, Cole. I'm a big girl. I didn't think we were getting married this afternoon."

"So I should return the engagement ring?"

"Yes. Return it and just give me the cash."

Good sense of humor. Didn't remember that about June. Maybe it was because Evan never shut his mouth long enough for her to speak. God, he was an asshole, and now I'm an asshole for sleeping with his wife less than two months after he was brutally murdered in a parking lot.

"I was going to call you," I said.

"I know. I just thought I would call you first to make you look like the bad guy."

"Ha-ha. Thanks for that."

"Don't mention it."

"So, are we supposed to see each other again?" I asked.

"I'm not sure. I would have to Google *one-night stand protocol.*"

"Okay, you do that, and if you're not busy this evening, maybe we could get dinner."

"Like a date, you mean?"

"I guess so."

"Okay, Cole. I'll look that up and get back to you this afternoon."

"Sounds like a plan, June. I'll talk to you later." I hung up the cell and grinned the rest of the way into work. I could feel myself slowly turning into the happy idiot.

Chapter Seventeen

"What the hell are you grinning about?" Leon asked when I walked through the kitchen door.

"I was just thinking about something," I replied.

"Obviously." Leon shut the cooler door and went to the freezer. "What's her name, boss?"

"You don't know her."

"Whatever."

I filled the mop bucket with hot water and floor cleaner and grabbed the mop. I wheeled the bucket into the men's room and began mopping. When I was finished with the men's room I went into the ladies room. I had the door propped open with the mop bucket. My back was to the door.

Allison stuck her head through the door. "Morning, Dad!"

"Jesus Christ! Don't do that. You scared the shit out of me."

She thought that was funnier than hell. "Sorry. I thought you heard me."

"Well, I didn't. You're here early."

"I woke up early. Couldn't get back to sleep. I was bored, so I came in."

Boredom, the Millennial generation's reason for working.

"What would you like for me to do?" Allison asked.

"Grab the blue bucket out of the supply closet," I told her, "and fill it with hot water and bleach, and clean the toilets in the ladies' room and the urinals in the men's."

"Ugh," she groaned. "You're punishing me for being early?"

I shook my head. "Yeah. That'll teach you."

Allison returned with the bucket just as I was finishing up the floor. She began scrubbing the inside of the toilet bowl. The expression on her face told the story of a young princess who was far too elegant to scrub toilets. "This is so gross," she said.

"You should have seen what I flushed down before you got here."

She made an over-exaggerated gagging sound. "Who usually does this?"

"Me."

"Maybe I need two more years of college."

"Or marry a wealthy man," I suggested.

She held the toilet brush gently with three fingers and daintily scrubbed way.

"Grab right a hold of that brush," I instructed. "Put some elbow grease into it." She ignored me. I thought about my, *marry a wealthy man,* comment. "Did you ever make plans with Spence?"

Allison dropped the brush back into the bucket. "We're supposed to go out to dinner tonight," she replied.

"Oh yeah?"

"Yeah." She picked up the bucket by its handle, walked past me, and headed toward the men's room. She paused and turned around. "I don't have to see him, ya know."

"What do you mean?"

"If it bothers you, I can cancel the date."

"Don't be silly," I said. "He's a good kid."

"Kid?"

"Man." I followed her to the other restroom. "You know who I saw this morning at breakfast?"

"I have no idea."

"Sherry Sprague."

Allison continued to work on the urinal. "Sherry Sprague? How did you see her?"

"She's working at Mulligan's in Jensen Beach. She's a waitress there."

"What were you doing in Jensen Beach?"

"I woke up early, couldn't sleep, and I was bored."

"Funny."

"You talk to her?"

"Yeah. She said to tell you she said hey."

"I probably haven't seen her in almost two years."

"I asked her if she knew Jimmy Bertran or Freddie Underwood."

"Oh yeah?"

"Yeah."

"Did she know either one of them?"

Allison's back was to me. I wished I had waited until she was facing me to bring up Freddie's name. I would like to have seen if the expression on her face changed at all. "She said she knew Freddie Underwood."

"Yeah, I think everyone our age knows him or knows of him."

"He probably purchased alcohol for most of you."

"She told you about that, did she?"

"Yup."

"We were just kids."

"Yup."

"Are you mad because I didn't tell you the whole truth?"

"Nope."

"Sorry. Letting some scumbag touch my boobs for beer isn't something I wanted to discuss with my dad."

"I don't blame you."

"You're not going to do anything to him, are you?"

"No, someone already took care of that."

She paused, dropped the brush in the water, and turned around. "What do you mean?"

"Someone broke into his trailer sometime Wednesday and killed him."

"Oh my God! That's horrible."

"It is."

"What happened?"

"What do you mean?"

"How was he killed?"

Part of me wanted to sugar-coat Freddie's death, because I didn't want my little girl to feel bad, but the father and cop in me wanted to scare the hell out of her and let her know how it ends for people like Freddie. "Someone broke into his trailer and bashed in his skull with something."

Allison winced. "Jesus."

"Yeah, Jesus."

"Do they have any leads?"

Spoken like a cop's daughter. "Not yet, but they will."

My cell phone rang. I looked at the number. It was June. "Hey," she said.

"Hi," I said.

"So, dinner tonight?"

"Sounds good to me."

"What time?"

"I'll pick you up at six."

"I'll be ready."

"See ya then." I hung up.

Allison stared at me with one eyebrow raised. "Who was that?" she asked.

"A friend."

"A friend who's a girl?"

"A friend who's a woman."

"You have a date?"

"Yes. Don't look so surprised."

"Well, you haven't been on a date in … a long time."

"Wow, I didn't know you kept track of that sort of thing."

"I do."

"And I have dated. I just don't talk to my daughter about it."

Allison picked up her cleaning bucket and squeezed between me and the door jamb. She was half-way down the hall when she stopped, and turned around. "It's not mom, is it?"

"What?"

"Your date. It's not with Mom is it?"

"Good God, no!"

Allison laughed. "Just making sure."

Chapter Eighteen

I pulled into June's driveway and glanced at the clock, 5:50. Never on time, never late, but always early—that's the way I roll. I opened my door and started to climb out of the truck, but June's front door opened and she walked out. She looked fantastic. She was dressed casual; I was a little nervous about that and was glad she dressed down, not up. I wasn't sure how wealthy women dressed for a first date with a poor man she had slept with the night before. I wondered if there was a book I could check out of the library that told all the rules for mid-life dating.

Oh shit, I thought, and quickly jumped out of the truck and met her at the passenger side door. I opened the door for her. I think it may have been the first time I had ever opened a car door for a lady—a lady other than a prostitute I was arresting, that is.

"You look wonderful," I said. *Wonderful?* That felt as uncomfortable as saying *good evening* the night before. *Stupid.* I should have just said, "You look great."

June smiled. "Thank you," she replied. "You look wonderful too."

I think she was mocking me a little bit.

I backed out of the driveway and started down the road. I glanced over at June's legs; they were fantastic, long and smooth, with nary a razor bump or spider vein to be seen. She looked even better than she had the night before. She wore white shorts with the ends frayed like cut-offs. Her tank top was almost exactly the same color as her skin—that is, sun kissed caramel. Over it, she wore a three-quarter sleeve, see-through top with a red flower print. The tank top had a built-in push-up bra that showcased Evan's birthday presents perfectly. On her feet were red pumps that matched the flowers on her top and her lipstick. June looked better than most woman half her age. She reminded me of a piece of candy shaped like a gorgeous woman—mouth-watering and completely edible.

I was wearing beige cargo shorts, brown deck shoes, and a light blue button-up shirt that I had picked up at Kohl's in Jensen Beach for a buck ninety-five. The shirt was regularly forty-nine dollars, but when I used my twenty dollars worth of Kohl's Cash along with the sale price, I had a two-dollar shirt. I love a good bargain. I wore the shirt untucked to hide the .38 revolver I had clipped to my belt. I figured my .357 was too big for a first date.

"So, where did you make reservations?" she asked.

"I didn't," I answered. "I've never been one for planning ahead."

"Evan was just the oppo—" She paused. "I'm sorry."

"Don't apologize. You can talk about anything you want to talk about."

"I do miss him."

"I know."

"Do you think it's okay what we're doing here?"

"Riding in a truck?"

"You know what I mean."

"We're two old friends going out to dinner."

"And sleeping together."

"We slept together once."

"But I'm sure we'll do it again," June said with a grin.

"I'm counting on it," I told her. "I wore brand new underwear tonight."

June laughed. "Me too."

I had wanted to go to The Original Tiki Bar & Restaurant—just the Tiki Bar to us locals—at the Fort Pierce Marina. But since Evan was murdered in a parking lot almost right across the street, I decided against it and drove to Duffy's Sports Grill in Stuart. I parked on the street and we sat at a table outside.

I ordered a Scotch on the rocks and June ordered a Mic Ultra. *Huh, Mic Ultra, so that's her secret.* I bet if I switched from Scotch to Mic Ultra every head would turn when I walked into a sports bar. Sure, it tastes like carbonated piss, but hey, that's just one of the sacrifices you make to be pretty.

When the waitress returned June ordered the chicken breast and I chose the fish tacos. Most of dinner was spent talking about Evan's climbing his way to the top of the real estate ladder, how much I enjoyed retirement and owning a bar, and what Lynn and June had been up to for the past thirteen years.

At one point I asked, "So, whatever happened to you and Lynn's friendship? You seemed very close for quite a few years."

"Some of it," she said, "had to do with you and Lynn's divorce. We didn't have the two of you to do things with as a couple, so we grew apart a little." June paused and stared out at the people walking down Osceola Street. "Evan had an affair around the same time."

"Oh," I said. "I didn't know that."

"Why exactly did you and Lynn split up?" June asked. "When I asked her about it she just said things weren't working out. She never explained what that meant."

"Well, she was right, things weren't working out. I never really knew why they weren't. One evening I got home from work and she said, 'I don't love you anymore. Either you have to leave or I do.' So, I left. I hadn't been happy for a while at that point, but I would have stayed and made it work anyway, for the sake of the kids. But Lynn wasn't the type to put the children's needs over her own."

I wanted to ask June why she and Evan never had children but I was afraid it might be a sore subject, so I let it go.

We each had another drink and finished our meals. We left the restaurant and walked down Osceola Street and back, and then we walked down Colorado Avenue. We stopped on the sidewalk at the corner of Colorado Avenue and Ocean Boulevard and kissed while we waited for a train to go by, and then went on. We held hands as we walked along.

We took a left on Sixth Street and came upon a bar called Terra Fermata. It was a funky place, a kaleidoscope of eye-popping color and festive lights, known for its craft beer and wine and live music every night under the stars. The scene reminded me of a wild block party in somebody's backyard. The hipster doofus at the gate nodded and said, "Hey," as we walked in. It was pretty much the same as the sports bar, in the way that every young guys head turned to get a look at June and her legs.

June sat in a lawn chair near a small stage where a young blond girl with dreadlocks sang Bob Dylan tunes. I waded through the sea of dancing bodies to the bar to get us a beer. June had asked for Mic Ultra, but I got her a Red Stripe instead.

We sat and talked and had a couple more beers. At one o'clock we decided that people our age should already be in bed. On our way out I heard someone say "Daddy?"

I turned around and saw Allison and Spence headed our way.

"Hello, Mrs. Walsh," Allison said with polite confusion. She turned to me. "What are you two doing here?"

"We were thirsty," I said.

Spence nodded. I nodded back.

"I thought you had a date tonight," said Allison. June and I looked at each other and then back at Allison. "Wait. Was your date with Mrs. Walsh?"

"Obviously," I said.

"Um, does Mom know?"

"No, and we would appreciate it if you didn't say anything," I said.

"Are you leaving?"

"Yes."

"Where are you going?"

"Back to my apartment."

"Why are you—oh. Okay."

"Well," I said, "I'll see you at work tomorrow."

"Um, yeah. See you at work."

"It was nice to see you, Allison," June said.

"Yeah, you too, Mrs. Walsh."

"Please, call me June."

"Oh," Allison said, turning to Spence. "This is Spence, my date. Spence, this is June … a friend of my mom's."

"It's nice to meet you, June," Spence said.

"You too, Spence."

I hugged Allison good bye, and June and I headed back across the train tracks to the truck. "That was uncomfortable," I remarked.

"Yes it was," June agreed.

We drove back to my place and June spent the night. I couldn't help stealing glances at her legs. And her breasts. And her … everything.

I could get used to this.

Chapter Nineteen

The following morning I ran to the store and grabbed a dozen eggs, bacon, bread, and a few other things, and made breakfast for June. After we ate we took our coffee into the living room and sat in front of the television. June was wearing my shirt from the night before. She looked way better in it than I did. That shirt was the best two bucks I ever spent. We made love on the couch, got dressed, and then I took her home.

When I returned to my apartment, I jumped in the shower, got dressed, and got to the bar at noon. Allison stared at me as I entered and made my way across the room toward the kitchen. I felt like I was doing the dreaded walk of shame.

"What?" I asked.

"Nothing," she replied.

"If you have something to say, say it."

"I don't have anything to say."

"Good."

Leon was in the kitchen prepping for lunch. "How was your night, boss?" he asked.

"Why, what did you hear?"

He looked up from the grill. "Nothing. Was I supposed to hear something?"

I walked back into the bar. "Bathrooms clean?" I asked.

"Yes," Allison answered.

"Who's here today?"

"Dalia, Norma, and me."

I stopped on my way out the side entrance. "You say anything about June to your mother?"

"You mean about her new boobs, or her new lips, or the work she's had done around her eyes?"

I continued on out the door. "Why did I ask?" I grumbled.

"No, I didn't say anything!" Allison shouted as the door shut behind me.

Kelly Morgan sat at one of the picnic tables sipping a Bud Light Lime. "You're late," he said.

"Late for what?" I asked.

"Lunch with me. Late night?"

I found it strange that no one ever asked me about my night until the one night I didn't want to talk about it. For now I would just like to keep it between me and June … and Spence and Allison. I would like to, but I couldn't.

"I got laid last night," I blurted out. "Twice ... and then again this morning." I was bragging like a high school kid, but I didn't care. June was great and I was falling for her.

"Um ... congratulations?" said Kelly.

I nodded and said "Thanks."

"Who's the semi-lucky girl?"

"June Walsh."

"June Walsh. Why does her name sound familiar? Wait, Walsh, the real-estate guy who was just murdered. Is that his wife?"

"Not *just* murdered, it was almost two months ago."

"Wow! That was one short mourning period."

"Shut up, dick head. What do you want for lunch?"

"Bacon cheeseburger and fries."

"I think I'll have the same thing," I went back inside. "Allison, grab me a Bud Light," I said as I walked past the bar. Spence was now sitting at the bar with her.

"You got it, lover boy," she replied.

Spence snickered.

"Enough!" I ordered. I stuck my head through the kitchen door. "Leon, can you make me two bacon cheeseburgers with fries?"

"Comin' right up, boss," Leon said.

"Thanks." I grabbed my beer on the way back through the bar. "Give me a holler when my food's up," I told Allison.

"Sure thing," she answered.

I sat down next to Kelly at the picnic table.

"So how did the two of you end up in the sack?" Kelly asked.

"I went to her house Friday night to ask her a few questions about her husband's death and one thing lead to another."

"Why were you asking her questions about her husband's murder?"

"My ex asked me to."

Kelly took a big swig of his beer. "I'm lost."

"Lynn, my ex, used to be friends with the Walshes. June mentioned to my ex that the investigation had stalled and wondered if I would ask a few questions and give the lead detective a call. So I did."

"And one thing lead to another."

"Exactly."

"So, what did you find out about the investigation?"

"Long story."

"I got all afternoon."

I spent the next few minutes filling Kelly in on what I had learned, and then Allison pushed open the side door. "Your order's up," she called out.

"Thanks," I said.

"You got it, lover boy."

Kelly laughed. "I take it Allison knows."

"Yeah. Her and Spence saw us at a bar together last night."

"Allison and Spence—what were they doing at a bar together? This place is like a soap opera: watch every day and nothing happens. Miss one day and you're lost."

"Spence and Allison went on a date last night too."

"So, when it comes to dating, all you Ballingers make your move at the same time."

I just shook my head and went back in to get our food.

When I returned I set Kelly's plate in front of him and my plate across from his. I took a seat on the other side of the table facing him and the water. Kelly was eager to jump right back into the conversation. "Are you gonna see her again?" he asked.

"I hope so," I replied. "I really like her. She's a lot of fun, and has a great sense of humor."

"A lot of fun in the sack?"

"It was really good. I haven't felt this way about a woman in a long time."

"What's your ex going to say when she finds out?"

"She's going to be pissed, but hey, she dumped me, I didn't dump her. Besides, Lynn and June have only seen each other a hand full of times in the last thirteen years. Lynn just recently tried to connect with her after the funeral. It didn't seem to me like June was all that eager to resume a friendship with Lynn."

"Lucky for you."

"That's what I thought. How long should I wait to give June a call, do you think?"

"You're asking me for relationship advice?" Kelly asked surprised.

"When you only have one friend, beggars can't be choosers."

"I'm honored."

"You should be. How long should I wait?"

"Who knows?"

"That's your advice—who knows?"

"Hey, what did you expect? I'm no expert when it comes to women. Remember, I'm single too. Maybe you should ask Spence, he seems to be doing pretty good."

"Watch it," I said. "That's my little girl."

Chapter Twenty

When I got to work on Monday morning I decided to go straight to my office and make a few phone calls. First I tried Angel's number. As usual, there was no answer, so I left a message. "Hey, baby," I said. "It's your dad. Hadn't heard from you in a few days. Thought I'd give you a call and see how you were doing. Talk to you later. Love ya." I hung up.

Angel not answering her phone was something I would never get used to. No matter how many times I called, the sound of her voice on the voice mail gave me a bad feeling in my gut. I never knew where she was. I never knew *how* she was. I just had to wait and hope she called back. She rarely did.

Next I dialed Tommy Franklin. "Hey, Tommy. It's Cole," I said.

"Hey, Cole. What's up?"

"Anything on the Underwood kid?"

"Nothing yet. CSI pulled about six or seven different sets of prints from the trailer. Most of his friends seem to have rap sheets so we matched all but two sets. Everyone had a pretty solid alibi for the time Underwood was killed. Neighbors weren't much help. Half the people in that park don't have jobs and are home all day, but none of them seen anything. There's a few people he works with that we still have to interview."

"Okay, Tommy, thanks. I'll get back to you if I hear anything."

"Thanks, Cole. Talk to you later."

I hung up and called June. "Hi, Cole," she answered.

"Hi, June. What are you doing?"

"Not much. I cleaned the pool this morning and then laid on the couch watching television for a while."

"You cleaned the pool? Don't you have a sexy pool boy for that?"

"Sounds like somebody's been watching too much vintage porn."

"Uh, well—"

"Your secret's safe with me. And you can be my sexy pool boy anytime." She paused and added in a suggestive purr: I wish you were lying next to me."

"Some of us have to work for a living."

"I remember those days. Didn't like working much," she said with a chuckle.

"If you get bored later and you're looking for something to do, stop by."

"The bar?"

"Sure."

"Okay. Maybe I will."

"I spoke with Detective Franklin a little bit ago."

"Oh yeah, what did he have to say?"

"Not much. We'll talk about it if you stop over, or I'll call you later."

"Okay," June said. "Talk to you later. Bye."

"Bye."

I had Jimmy Bertran's number and thought about giving him a call, but I didn't. I decided maybe I would just stop by Subway later and talk to him if I had a chance. I should have asked Tommy if one of the sets of finger prints was Jimmy's, but I didn't think of it. I figured I would call him back before I went to talk to the kid. My mind seemed to be more on my two evenings spent with June than Evan's murder.

I thought about calling C.J., but it was always a hassle. If I wanted to talk to him I had to call the house. His mother always answered the phone and then I had to ask permission to speak to my own son. That was always followed by questions. What did I want? Why hadn't I called in so long? His mother didn't think he was old enough for a cell phone even though all of his friends had one as well as everyone else his age. I tried to buy him one once and that lead to a bunch of bullshit about going behind Lynn's back and me not respecting her rules. I decided not to call.

The phone on my desk rang and I picked it up. "Breakwater Bar and Grill. How can I help you?"

"You goddamn son of a bitch!" Lynn hollered.

"Hi, Lynn."

"Don't you 'Hi, Lynn' me, you piece of shit!"

There's the Lynn I know and don't love. "You sound angry," I said.

"Oh, you think you're so smart, you bastard."

Wow! Bastard, piece of shit, and son of a bitch in less than two minutes. This might be a record for Lynn. "Calm down, Lynn. What's the matter?"

"You know very well what the matter is. How long have you been screwing her?"

"Not long."

"So, you admit it?"

"Of course I admit it. We've been divorced for almost fifteen years, Lynn, I don't think we need to ask each other who we're allowed to date."

"Oh, so you're dating."

"Kind of. Who told you about it?"

"It doesn't matter who told me. How long has this been going on?"

"A couple days."

"I never should have asked you to look into Evan's death. I guess this is all my fault."

"It's no one's fault, Lynn, it just happened."

"I thought she was my friend."

I didn't know what to say to that. Lynn and June *weren't* friends. They *used* to be friends, but they had barely seen each other in years. June didn't seem like she was even interested in being Lynn's friend. It was a one-sided friendship and I knew it, but I couldn't tell Lynn that.

"What do you want me to do, Lynn?" I asked.

"I want you to stop seeing her."

"I'm not going to do that."

"You'll regret this!"

"I am right now."

Lynn slammed the phone down without saying goodbye. I dialed June's number again, but it went straight to voicemail.

"June, it's Cole again. I just got a call from Lynn. Someone told her about us. Just giving you a heads-up. She might be calling you next … if she hasn't already. Call me back if you want." I hung up the phone. *Shit!* I didn't think Lynn would find out this quickly.

I got up from my desk and went to the bar to warn Allison. She was on the phone and glaring at me when I rounded the corner.

"I know, Mom," Allison said. "I know … no, Mom." She dropped her head down and stared at the floor. "I'm not on his side, Mom. I'm not on anyone's side."

I went behind the bar and got myself a glass, filled it with ice, and added ginger ale. I walked back around the bar and sat on one of the stools. When Allison finally hung up her cell phone, I asked, "Something wrong?"

"That's great, Dad, make a joke."

"Sorry. What am I supposed to do?"

Allison shrugged. "I don't know."

"How did she find out?"

"She didn't say."

"Someone must have seen us at the bar or at Duffy's."

"You want me to stock the beer cooler?" Allison asked, changing the subject.

I downed my soda and climbed off the stool. "I'll get it. Oh, and June is probably stopping by here this afternoon."

"So this is going to be a regular thing with you two?"

"I don't know; we haven't talked about it. We're just playing it by ear. Are you okay with this?"

"*I'm* fine. You're both adults. Just make sure you wear a condom and if you have any questions about sex, just ask."

I shook my head. "That's real cute."

Chapter Twenty-One

Around four o'clock Tommy Franklin stopped in. "Well, look at you," he said, when he spotted me behind the bar. "So this is what we do after we retire?"

"This is it," I replied, as I looked around the room with my hands on my hips pretending to survey all that was mine.

"Looks boring."

I glanced over at Melvin; his shoulders shook at Tommy's remark.

"Boring? You call this boring?"

Tommy scanned the room. Melvin and one other guy sat at the bar. The jukebox quietly played *Good Shepherd* by Jefferson Airplane. "Yes, *very* boring." He grabbed a stool in the middle of the bar.

"What'll ya have?" I asked, trying my best to sound like a stereotypical Old-West saloon owner.

"Coors Light," Tommy replied.

Talk about boring. I grabbed him a beer and twisted off the top. "There you go."

Tommy reached for his wallet.

"On me," I said.

Of course it is," Melvin grumbled.

Tommy pulled out his wallet anyway and said, "Get these two guys whatever they're drinking and get one for yourself."

Melvin and the other guy raised their glasses. "Thank you," they both said.

"So, what brings you in, Tommy?" I asked.

Tommy leaned into me. "You got somewhere we can talk?"

"Sure. Just let me grab someone to replace me back here. There was something I wanted to ask you too."

I ran into the kitchen and asked Emily to jump behind the bar, and then Tommy and I walked out to the picnic tables. We sat on opposite sides, me facing the water.

"What is it, Tommy?" I asked.

"How well did you know Evan Walsh?"

"Like I said, I kinda grew up with him. He was a couple years behind me in school but he was one of those kids who always seemed to be around, even if you didn't want him around. He was always a big pain in the ass."

"When was the last time you saw him ... before the night he was killed, I mean?"

I thought for a second. "It had to have been eleven or twelve years."

"What about Lynn?"

"What about her?"

"When was the last time she spoke with him?"

"I have no idea. Probably not in years. She and June were friends for a while, years ago, but around the time of our divorce they stopped speaking."

"Do you know why they stopped speaking?"

"I asked June that same question. She said that around the time Lynn and I divorced, she and Evan were having problems of their own."

"What kind of problems?"

"I guess Evan had had an affair. Why are you asking me all of these questions and not June?"

"We searched through Walsh's cell phone records and found out he was having an affair with two different women at the time of his murder."

"Wow, June didn't mention that."

"And she claimed to have no knowledge of it when *I* asked her."

"Maybe she didn't know."

"There were also three calls placed to your ex-wife's house in the two weeks leading up to Walsh's death."

"Seems like there's a lot of things people aren't telling me. Were there any calls *from* Lynn's home *to* Walsh's cell?"

"None."

"How long did the calls last?"

"The first two were under three minutes, but the last call—three nights before he died—lasted around twenty minutes."

"Have you questioned Lynn about this?"

"Not yet. I wanted to give you a heads-up."

"Did you mention to June the calls from Evan's cell to Lynn?"

"I didn't think it was necessary at this point."

"Thanks, Tommy. You do what you have to do."

"What was it you wanted to ask me?"

"The fingerprints—were any of them Jimmy Bertran's?"

"The other kid who works at the sub shop?"

"Yeah."

"No, but we have two sets we haven't matched yet."

I heard the door open behind me, and saw Tommy's brow drop. I turned around. It was June. She kept a straight face as she walked toward me.

"Mrs. Walsh," Tommy said.

"Detective Franklin," June said.

Tommy looked at me and then back at June.

"Are you looking for me?" Tommy asked.

"No," June said. "I stopped by to speak with Cole. I was wondering if he had made any progress with Evan's investigation."

"Have a seat, June," I said, and scooted over.

"Thank you, Cole."

"But since you are here, Detective Franklin, how is everything going with the case?"

"We're working on some leads," Tommy said vaguely. He got up from the table. "I'll leave you two to discuss whatever it is you need to discuss."

I stood too and walked Tommy around the building to the street. When we got to Tommy's car he turned and said, "I hope you know what you're doing, Cole."

"What do you mean?"

"She's a beautiful woman."

"I've noticed."

We shook hands and I thanked Tommy for stopping by. I watched as he drove his car around the park and headed back down Seaway Drive, then I returned to the picnic table and sat across from June.

"What did he say?" June asked.

"About what?"

She cocked her head and smirked. "What do you think?"

"About us?"

"Yes."

"He said you were a beautiful woman."

"The keen eye of a police detective."

"We have someone else to worry about anyway."

"Oh yeah? Who?"

"Lynn."

"Why do you say that?"

"She knows about us. She called this morning. I figured she had called you too."

"She didn't call me."

"Did you know that she had spoken to Evan at least three times in the two weeks leading up to his death?"

"Who told you that?"

"Franklin. He said there were three calls. The first two lasted less than three minutes, but the third call lasted more than twenty. The last call was three nights before he died."

"Why would he have called her?"

"I don't know, June, I was hoping you knew."

"Well, I don't. Can I get a drink, Cole?"

"A beer?"

"I think I need something a little stronger. Scotch might do the trick."

"Sure," I said, and went to get her a drink. When I returned I sat the glass in front of her and then watched her take a few sips.

"Why didn't Detective Franklin ask me about the phone calls?" June asked. "I've spoken with him at least a half a dozen times in the last few weeks."

"Tommy's not the type of guy to show his entire hand until he has to."

"Has he asked Lynn about it?"

"Not yet, but he's going to. That's why he was here, he wanted to give me a heads-up." I reached out and took hold of June's hands. "June, did you know Evan was having affairs?"

She let go of one of my hands and swallowed a big swig of Scotch this time. "I told you he had an affair."

"I meant recently."

"Did Franklin tell you that too?"

I nodded my head. "Yeah."

"What did he say?"

"He said Evan was having affairs with two different women at the time of his death."

June took a deep breath, held it for a few seconds, and then exhaled. "Of course I knew, Cole."

"Franklin said you told him you knew nothing about it."

"I didn't want him to think I was a fool."

"Because Evan was having an affair?"

"Because I let it go on."

"How long was it going on?"

June stared over my shoulder at the water. "It went on all the time. He always had girlfriends. The first time I found out we almost separated. He swore it would never happen again. A few years later it happened again. And then again and again. Each time we fought less about it and after a while it was just the norm."

"When was the first time?"

"The time I told you about. Around the time you and June separated." A tear ran down June's cheek and she sniffed. She wiped the lone tear away with the back of her hand.

"Are you hungry?" I asked.

She shook her head no and rubbed her eyes. "I think I'm going to go home."

June got up from the table, walked around to my side, and kissed me on the cheek.

"You don't have to leave," I told her. "You can stay if you want to."

"I know. Thank you. These last few days have been really nice, Cole. I haven't felt like this in a long time." She turned my head and kissed me on the lips. "I'll call you later tonight."

"Okay."

"What should I say if Lynn does call me?" June asked.

"Tell her the truth."

June smiled, turned, and walked to her car.

Chapter Twenty-Two

At six o'clock the door opened and in walked C.J. and a friend.

"Hey, kid," I said with a big smile.

"Hi, Dad," he replied, and then motioned toward his buddy. "You remember Carl Anderson."

"Yeah," I said. "How're you doing, Carl?"

"Good, Mr. Ballinger," Carl answered.

I met C.J. at the end of the bar. We hugged and I gave him a kiss on top of the head. "Long time, no see," I said.

"Yeah," he responded.

"So, what are you guys up to tonight?"

"I'm spending the night at Carl's house," C.J. informed me. "He lives right over on Binney Drive so we rode our bikes over."

The boys climbed aboard two of the barstools.

"Soda?" I asked.

"Yes, please," Carl said.

I poured them each a drink and set the sodas on the bar in front of them. "Hungry?" I asked.

"We just had wings next door," C.J. said.

"We have wings here too, ya know," I told him.

"Theirs are better."

"Great."

"Did you hear they're putting a TGI Friday's down the street?" C.J. asked.

"Yeah."

"That's gonna be awesome."

"Yeah, awesome," I said. "Can't wait."

C.J. and his friend drank their sodas and we talked about the Rays being in first place in the American League. We talked about what his plans were for summer vacation. C.J. told me he had asked his mom if he could wash dishes at The Breakwater a few nights a week. She told him she would think about it, and we both knew that probably meant no. I promised him I would speak to her about it.

The two boys each had a second soda and ate some potato chips. Then C.J. said they had to get going, that they were meeting some other boys out on the jetty to go fishing. We hugged and I told him I loved him. He didn't say it back in front of his friend but I knew he loved me too.

"Bye. Be careful," I said, and they were out the door.

"Fine boy ya got there, Cole," said Melvin.

"Thanks, Melvin," I said.

Melvin slid his empty glass across the bar and said, "Well, I better be off."

"See you tomorrow," I said.

Melvin walked out the door and the bar was empty. I walked back to the kitchen.

"How's it going back here, Leon?" I asked.

"Pretty slow, boss," he replied. "Anybody in the dining room?"

"Nope, the place is empty." Monday nights—hell, Mondays period—were usually pretty slow, but it was still discouraging because I knew TGI Friday's would soon be hopping no matter what night of the week it was.

As I walked back into the bar, Norma came in from outside. "This place is dead," she said.

"Yeah. Why don't you go ahead and cut Dalia."

"You got it."

I waited until around nine o'clock and told Norma I was going to take off. I told her to close up if it was still empty at ten. My plan was to stop by Subway and speak with Jimmy Bertran if he was there, and if he wasn't, maybe stop by his house.

I was halfway across the park on my way to my truck when two young men stepped into the path in front of me. I nodded. "Hey, guys," I said. "What's up?"

Neither spoke at first, they just stood their ground. As I neared, the one nearest me pulled a knife from behind his back. I froze and put my hands up in front of me.

The other kid was wearing a thin windbreaker; he had his hand shoved into the right pocket. He wanted me to think he had a gun. I was pretty sure he didn't. Gun barrels are a little bigger than the average finger and aren't rounded at the tip.

"Whoa, guys," I said. "Let's think about this for a second."

"Give us the money, man," said the kid with the knife.

"What money?" I asked calmly.

The moon was full and bright and I could see the nervous looks on their faces. I wondered if they knew it would be a full moon when they planned this.

"The money from the register. We know you own that bar back there," said the kid in the windbreaker.

"I don't have the money from the register. All I have on me is my wallet ... and you're not getting it."

They looked at each other and then back at me.

"Turn around slowly," said the kid with the knife. "We'll walk back to the bar and get the money out of the register."

"No," I said.

He made a couple of laughable thrusting motions with the knife. "Man, you better do as I say or I'll gut you like a fish."

"No, *man*, you're going to do as *I* say," I told him. "Or I'm going to hurt you and your friend."

Windbreaker grinned nervously. "Hurt *us*?"

"Yes. Now, you lay the knife on the ground, and you take your hand out of your pocket."

Knife Boy lunged at me with a slashing motion. I leaned back and the blade passed inches in front of my chest. It would be his only opportunity—he should have thrusted instead of slashed.

I stepped toward him and grabbed his wrist with my right hand and his shoulder with my left. I yanked his arm downward as hard as I could as I brought up my knee into his elbow. In the quiet of the evening the sickening sound of breaking bone seemed almost deafening. He cried out in pain as the knife dropped from his grip.

Windbreaker's eyes widened and he took two steps back.

I looked down at his pocket; his hand was shaking.

I put a foot behind Knife Boy and tripped him to the ground. He fell on his back holding his arm and moaning.

"Well, are you going to shoot that finger?" I asked.

He pulled his hand from his pocket, turned, and took off running. He only made it about thirty feet before I tackled him.

Windbreaker was on his stomach and I was on top of him. He brought his elbow around and got me in the cheek.

"Ow, you little bastard!" I shouted.

He tried to crawl out from under me.

I rose up and flipped him over.

He swung at me.

I grabbed him by the front of the jacket and picked him up. When he was on his feet I stepped back and hit him in the face with a right, then a left, and then another right. He stumbled back a few steps, fell to his ass, and then onto his back. He was out cold.

I looked back over my shoulder at the other guy. He was still holding his arm. I thought I could hear him crying.

I reached down and brushed the grass off of my knees; they were scraped and bloody. My cheek hurt; so did my back and my shoulder. I knew I would be in a lot more pain tomorrow. Shit, I hate getting old.

I grabbed my cell phone and called 911. I gave the woman at the other end my name, told her I was standing in the middle of Jetty Park, and gave her a brief description of what had taken place.

"Was there a weapon involved in the altercation?" she asked.

"There was a knife," I told her. "But I'm now in possession of it."

"Are the two men who attacked you still in the area?"

"Yes. One is unconscious and the other is rolling around on the ground whimpering like a little bitch."

"Do you need me to dispatch an ambulance?"

I was done talking in circles and repeating myself, so I hung up, put my phone back in my pocket, and took a seat on a nearby bench.

"Hey!" I called out to the kid with the broken arm.

"What?"

"An ambulance is on its way."

"Fuck you, man," he moaned.

I got up from the bench and ambled over to where the punk lay. "Well, son," I said, "since you haven't learned to respect your elders, it's time you learned to respect your betters."

Knife boy looked up at me with defiant eyes. "What the hell's that supposed to mean, old man?"

"Just a little quote I borrowed from John Wayne."

"John Wayne? Who that, your lover?"

I ground my foot into the broken arm and took more pleasure than I should have in the scream that split the night.

"That was for being a snot-nosed little prick ... *and* for not knowing who John Wayne is."

Chapter Twenty-Three

By the time I gave the cops my statement and the young hooligans were hauled away it was after midnight, so I climbed in my truck and drove home. When I got there I found Angel lying in the doorway to my apartment. I froze for a second, waiting to see some kind of movement. She breathed in and I was relieved.

I knelt down beside her and brushed the hair away from her face. "Angel," I said.

Her eyelids opened. Her eyes were glassy and couldn't focus.

"Daddy," she replied.

I put my hands under her arms. "Can you get up, princess?" I asked.

She did her best to help me help her to her feet. I put her arm around my neck and my arm around her waist. I pulled the house keys from my pocket with my other hand and unlocked the door.

I got her to the couch and sat her down. She lay down with her head on the armrest and closed her eyes. I grabbed a blanket from the spare bedroom and put it over her.

I got a beer out of the fridge and returned to the living room. I turned on the television and turned the volume down almost all the way. I sat down at the other end of the couch, kicked off my shoes, and stared at the television. I felt myself dozing off just moments into Stephen Colbert's opening monologue.

At 1:30 my cell phone's irritating buzzing jarred me awake; it was Lynn. "Yeah?" I said.

"You're a piesh a shit. You know that?" she said. She was obviously drunk.

"So I've been told," I responded.

"She's *my* friend."

"She's not your friend, Lynn. She *was* your friend … years ago."

"You has a answer for airthing."

I knew C.J. was staying at a friend's house. "Is Allison at home?" I asked.

"No. I'm alone. I'm always alone."

"That's not my fault, Lynn." I glanced over at Angel to make sure she was still asleep.

"Everyone leaves me," Lynn said.

"Why don't you get some sleep? We'll talk in the morning."

"Yeah, that's what you do. Just brush me off. You think you're so smart. You think you know airthing. I could tell you a few things, mister."

"I'm sure you could." The conversation was getting old quickly. I wanted to hang up, but I was a little nervous what Lynn might do once I did.

"You men are all alike. You ... Evan. You're all alike. Liars!"

"What are you talking about, Lynn? Who lied to you?"

"Never mind," she said. "I could tell you a thing or something."

"Lynn, did you talk to Evan a few nights before he was killed?"

"Ha! He thinks he's so smart. You all think you're so smart. He got what he deserved."

"What do you mean, Lynn?" I waited for a response but the call ended. "Lynn!" Nothing. "Dammit!"

I called Kelly Morgan's number.

"Hello?" he grumbled.

"Kelly, it's me," I said.

"What?"

"It's Cole."

"Cole?"

"Kelly, are you awake? It's Cole."

"It's almost two in the morning," he informed me.

"Kelly, I need you to come to my apartment."

"What's the matter?" He was sounding more alert.

"Angel is here and I don't want to leave her by herself. I need to go over to Lynn's. Can you come over here?" I wedged my cell phone between my shoulder and my ear and talked as I tied my sneakers.

"Yeah."

"I'm leaving now. I'll leave the front door unlocked, just get here as quick as you can."

"I'm leaving now."

"Thanks." I hung up, went out the door, and jumped into my truck.

At two in the morning it was only a five-minute drive from my apartment to Lynn's house on Weatherbee Road. When I arrived I ran up to the door and tried the knob; it was locked. I pounded on the door with my fist. "Lynn!" I hollered. Just as I expected there was no answer, but I yelled again any way. "Lynn!"

I threw my shoulder into the door—the shoulder I had injured earlier in the night—and winced in pain. I backed up and kicked as hard as I could just to the left of the doorknob, splintering the jamb. The door swung open violently and hit the wall behind it.

"Lynn!" I ran to the living room and then the bed room.

Lynn lay on the bed on her back in her bathrobe. An empty bottle of Merlot sat on the nightstand next to an open bottle of Vicodin. I grabbed the container, it was empty. I dialed 911, and then sat down beside her.

I slapped her cheek. "Lynn, wake up!"

"Emergency services. How can I help you?"

"This is Cole Ballinger, I'm at 1104 Weatherbee Road. I have an unresponsive, forty-seven year old female who may have ingested several Vicodin."

"An ambulance is on the way, sir. Can you stay on the line?"

I slapped Lynn again. "Wake up, Lynn! Wake up!" I set my phone down on the night stand, grabbed her by the shoulders with both hands, and shook her. "Lynn!"

I put my ear to her chest; her heartbeat was there, but faint, and her breathing was shallow.

It was only another minute or two until I heard the blaring sirens. I scooped Lynn up into my arms and ran for the door.

I got to the front door as the ambulance was backing down the driveway.

The doors of the ambulance swung open and the paramedics jumped out and ran to the back of the vehicle. One of them opened the rear doors and climbed inside.

"She's breathing and I got a faint heart beat," I said.

"Do you know how many she took?" the driver asked.

"I have no idea. I was on the phone with her about twenty minutes ago. She sounded drunk but I don't know if she had already taken the pills or not. She was drinking red wine."

"They usually take the pills *after* they make the call," the driver said.

I lifted Lynn up to the other paramedic and he laid her on the gurney.

The driver slammed one of the doors but held the other open. "You riding with us?" he asked.

"No, I'll meet you there."

The ambulance pulled away, and I went to shut the damaged front door as best I could. As I ran back to my truck, I reached for my phone and dialed.

"Hello?" said Spence.

I backed out of the driveway and headed down Weatherbee. I could see the flashing lights of the ambulance in the distance. "Spence, it's Cole."

"Is everything okay, Cole?"

"No. Is Allison with you?"

"Um ... I, uh—"

"Is she with you, or not, Spence?"

"Yes, Cole, but we're not doing—"

"Shut up, Spence, and listen to me. It's Allison's mom. She took some pills. They're taking her to Lawnwood Medical. I'll meet you there."

"Okay, Co—"

I hung up the cell and laid it in the center console.

I took a deep breath and slowly exhaled. *What a night.*

Chapter Twenty-Four

A few minutes after four that morning the doctor on call walked into the waiting room and told us that Lynn would be just fine. Allison broke down and cried. I turned to her but Spence was quicker; he put his arm around Allison and she buried her face in his chest.

Dr. Burke looked at me and said, "She's asking to see you, Cole." I got up and followed the doctor down the hall to Lynn's room.

Burke pushed the door open and stepped aside. "Here ya go," he said. "She's still a little out of it."

Lynn lay in the bed with her head slightly elevated. Tubes ran from the back of her hand to two IV bags hanging above her bed. Wires ran from under her gown, out through the neck hole to an EKG monitor. Her eyes were closed.

I walked up beside the bed and put my hand on hers. Her eyelids fluttered and then slowly opened.

"Cole," she said.

I pulled my hand back. "Lynn."

"I'm sorry, Cole."

"Don't apologize. The doctor said you're going to be fine. Probably go home later this afternoon. I sort of convinced him and the EMTs it was an accident."

"But we know better, don't we, Cole?" She turned her head toward the window. It was still dark. The only light outside came from the amber glow of street lights.

"Lynn, what did you mean when you said, 'He got what he deserved'?"

She continued to stare out the window. "Who?" she asked.

"When we were on the phone last night you said that Evan Walsh got what he deserved."

"Did I? I don't know why I would have said that."

"I don't either, Lynn. That's why I'm asking."

She shrugged her shoulders.

"Do you know something about Evan's death?" I asked.

"How would I know anything?"

"Why was Evan calling you?"

"Who said he called me?"

"Tommy Franklin. They looked through Evan's phone records, Lynn. Evan called you three times, the last time being three nights before he was killed."

Lynn closed her eyes. "I don't know. I'm tired."

"Lynn, if you know something you have to tell me."

"I can't," she whispered.

A nurse entered the room.

"Lynn," I said, and shook her arm. "Lynn."

There was no response.

"Lynn."

The nurse stepped up beside me. "Why don't we let your wife get some rest, Mr. Ballinger."

I turned and walked toward the door. "She's not my wife," I said. I left the room, headed down the hall, and when I returned to the waiting room June was seated next to Allison.

June stood when she saw me. "Is she going to be alright?" she asked.

Allison turned her head toward me.

"The doctor said she's going to be fine," I told them.

"Thank God," said June.

"Can I see her?" Allison asked.

"She's sleeping, but I think it'd be all right if you went in," I said.

Allison got up and walked down the hall.

I sat down next to June. "Thanks for coming," I said.

"Well, when you called me," June said, "I thought … I mean, I just wanted to be with you." She took my hand, pulled it up next to her mouth, and kissed it.

I didn't know how to reply to that, so I just smiled and nodded my head. I sat back in the chair, crossed my legs, and stared at the television mounted on the wall across the room.

Spence got up. "I saw a coffee machine down the hall. I think I'll grab myself a cup," he said. "Can I get you a cup, Cole?"

"Yeah, Spence, that would be great, thanks."

"How about you, June?" he asked.

"Yes, please," said June.

Spence turned and left the room.

I watched as June scanned the waiting area. She had an odd look on her face.

"What's the matter?" I asked.

"I was just thinking, the last time I was here was the night Evan was killed," she replied.

"Are you okay?"

"Yes." June paused for a second. "Cole, you never told me why you were here that night … the night they brought Evan in."

"The hospital staff phoned me. They said they couldn't reach you and they found my old business card in Evan's wallet."

"Were you home when they called you?"

"No, I was at the bar. Why?"

"I just wondered how you got here so fast. I wish I had gotten here before he died. I had gone to bed and the ringer on my phone was off. Did he say anything to you?"

"Say anything? What do you mean?"

"Anything about me," she replied. "I don't know, I guess I was just wondering what his last words were. I know, it's crazy."

"It's not crazy. He squeezed my hand and said he was sorry."

"Sorry? Huh."

Spence returned with the three Styrofoam cups of coffee and handed June and me ours. We muttered our thanks.

The three of us sat and nursed the hot brew in silence for about fifteen minutes and then Allison returned; she looked better than when she left.

"They said she'll sleep for the next few hours," Allison said. "I think I'll run home and take a shower and get changed and then come back over."

"Stay with her, Spence," I said. "I had to kick the front door open and it won't latch now, so I don't want her to be there alone."

"Sure thing," Spence said. "I've already called in and took a personal day for tomorrow." He got up and shook my hand, and then he and Allison left.

"That Spence seems like a nice kid," June said.

"He is," I said. "We might as well get out of here too. You want to come back to my place?"

June grinned. "I better not. I need to get a couple hours of sleep."

"I put my arms around her. "We can just sleep if you want."

"That's the problem," she said. "Once I get there I won't want to just sleep."

"Yeah, I know what you mean. I'm pretty irresistible."

Chapter Twenty-Five

June drove back to her place and I drove back to mine. I figured I would wait a few hours and then drive over to C.J.'s friend's house and tell him about his mother. No sense in waking him up.

When I walked through my front door, Angel was still lying on the couch asleep, her greasy blonde hair strewn across her face. Kelly was sitting in the recliner, also sound asleep.

"Hey," I said.

He opened his eyes and looked around. "How did everything go?" he asked, as he stretched his arms above his head.

"She's fine. She's in the hospital."

He yawned. "But she's fine."

"Yup." I nodded my head toward Angel. "Anything out of sleeping beauty?" I asked.

"She turned over a couple times, but she never really woke up."

"Thanks for coming over."

"Anytime, pal. Besides, who else would you call? You haven't got any other friends."

"What time do you have to be to work?"

Kelly looked at his watch. "Twenty minutes ago."

"You want a cup of coffee?"

"No, thanks. I'll grab one on the way."

Kelly got up and left, and I went into the kitchen to start a pot of coffee. I wanted to take a shower, but I was afraid Angel would be gone when I got out, so I sat at the kitchen table and flipped through a recent issue of AARP's magazine. Another detective had signed me up for a subscription as a joke around the time I retired. The joke was on him, it was a pretty good magazine. I was just starting an article about Cyndi Lauper still having fun after all these years when Angel entered the kitchen.

"Hey, princess," I said.

"Morning, Daddy," she replied.

"Hungry?"

"Starving."

She had a small scab on her lip and a fading bruise above her left eye. Her hair looked as though it hadn't been washed in weeks. The old pair of gray sweatpants she had on had a hole in one of the knees; her T-shirt was filthy and reeked of BO. Her arms were painfully thin and looked tanned at first glance, but then I realized they were just brown with grime. I stared probably a moment too long at her face; the gauntness reminded me of something.

Suddenly I knew what it was: a skeleton mask she wore for Halloween when she was a kid. Happy times. A million years ago.

"Why don't you jump in the shower and I'll make you some breakfast. There's some of your sister's jeans and a few T-shirts in the drawer in the spare bedroom."

"Can you make pancakes?"

"I can."

Angel smiled, walked over and gave me a kiss on the cheek, and said, "Thank you, Daddy."

"No problem, baby."

She disappeared down the hall. I got up and went to the cupboard for the pancake mix.

As I poured the batter onto the electric griddle and waited for the air bubbles to form on the pancakes I could hear the blow dryer coming from the bathroom. A few seconds after the hair dryer shut off, Angel walked back into the kitchen. She was wearing a pair of Allison's jeans and a long sleeved flannel shirt with the sleeves rolled up. The pants and shirt were noticeably too large for her small frame, but her hair was done, she was clean, and she looked beautiful. She looked like my little girl.

"Coffee?" I asked.

"Sure," she replied, stepping over to the cabinet and grabbing herself a mug.

"There's milk in the fridge and the sugar is over the stove."

"I take it black," she said as she poured the coffee into the cup. Then she sat down at the table. She slid my magazine over in front of her and smiled. "Reading your old man magazine?" she asked.

"Yup. That's what we old-timers do."

"Do you watch *Matlock* and *Murder, She Wrote* now too?"

"I'm more of a *Golden Girls* type of guy." I scooped up two of the pancakes and placed them on a plate. "You want butter on these?"

"Just syrup. Hey, you got any Mrs. Butterworth's? That was always my favorite."

I remembered. "Mine, too." I grabbed the plump grandma-shaped bottle out of the cupboard and placed it along with her plate on the table in front of her. I set a fork and a napkin next to the plate. She wolfed down the pancakes as though she hadn't eaten in days. I poured more batter onto the skillet to make three more.

"These are so good," Angel said. She crammed the last bite into her mouth.

"I can tell," I said. "Three more coming right up."

When the next three pancakes were done I put them on her plate and she devoured them just as fast as the first two. After she was all done eating she carried her coffee into the living room and sat down on the couch. She pulled her legs up under her, grabbed the remote control, and began flipping through the stations. I unplugged the skillet, and placed Angel's dish and fork into the sink. After I wiped down the table and counter top I joined her on the couch.

"What are you watching?" I asked.

"There's nothing on," she replied, and stopped on an old repeat of *Roseanne*.

"There never is," I agreed.

We sat together and watched television for about fifteen minutes without saying a word. We would glance at each other and laugh at each joke. My mind wandered back to a time when I would sit on the couch with my girls and watch old cartoons on the Boomerang Channel. While other children were watching *Rugrats*, *Hey Arnold!*, and *SpongeBob Square Pants,* me and my kids were watching old episodes of *The Pink Panther* and *Bugs Bunny*. I loved being a dad back then. You have nothing to worry about when your kids are sitting next to you on the couch watching cartoons.

I glanced down at the clock on the cable box.

"Hey," I said. "I have to drive over to the Anderson's and pick up your brother. You want to ride along?"

"No," Angel replied. "I better get going."

"Your mom had a little accident last night and she's in the hospital."

Angel's head spun around. "Accident? Is she okay?"

"She's fine. They're letting her go home this afternoon. I just wanted to pick up your brother and take him over to see her this morning. Why don't you come along? She would love to see you."

Angel cocked her head. "I bet she would," she said sarcastically.

"Ride over with me."

"I have a lot of things to do today. I'll stop over and see her later, or I'll run by the house."

"Are you sure?"

"I'm positive. Can you drop me off somewhere on your way?"

"Yeah."

"Daddy, can I borrow a couple bucks?" Angel asked in the same sweet tone she used as a little girl. Back then I could never say no, today it was a different story.

"Borrow?" I asked. "For what?"

"I need a few things from the drug store."

"Like what?"

"Personal things, and I need to pick up my birth control."

"I'll go in with you and pay for the things you need, but I'm not giving you any money."

Angel became agitated. "I'm not going to have my father come in and pay for those things for me."

"Then you won't be getting them."

"Why do you have to be so difficult? I need my birth control. Do you want me to end up pregnant? It would be your fault." Her voice grew louder as she became more aggressive.

"Nothing you do is *my* fault. Your mother and I agreed not to give you any more money. Now, do you want me to pay for those things or not?"

"Forget it. I'll ask Ted for the money. He cares about what happens to me."

"Does he? Did Ted care enough to put that cut on your lip, or the bruise over your eye? Does Ted care enough to make sure you have a decent meal every day or a clean place to live, or nice clothes to wear?"

Angel just sat there and glared at me. In her mind I was in the wrong. "Can you drop me off at the liquor store, or not?"

"Sure," I said. "Let me change my clothes and wash up."

Ted Hale's Plymouth Duster was parked out front of the liquor store when I dropped Angel off. Before the truck came to rest, Angel opened the door. She jumped out as I stopped without saying a word.

"I love you," I called out.

"Sure you do," she hollered back over her shoulder.

I drove to the Andersons' house and picked C.J. up. On the way to the hospital I explained to him exactly what had happened the night before. I changed the story a bit to make it more fourteen-year-old-boy friendly. I told him that his mom had misread the label and taken too much medication—same thing I told the EMTs and the doc. That, along with the glass of wine she drank made her light headed and she called me just before she passed out.

I let C.J. go in and visit his mom by himself; I didn't want to see her. Afterwards I asked him how she was doing. He just said "Good." I asked him if he wanted to spend the night at my place and he told me he would rather stay at home with his mother in case she needed anything. I agreed.

After I dropped C.J. back at the Anderson's I called a guy—Lance Cane—who had done some work for me at the bar and asked him if he could run out to Lynn's place and fix the front door. He said he could.

As soon as I ended my call with Lance, Allison called me and said she wouldn't be in for work. I told her I had figured she wouldn't be.

Chapter Twenty-Six

"You look like shit," Norma said as I walked into the bar.

"You should see the other guy," I returned.

"I saw the other guys," she said, "laying out in the park."

Oh yeah, I thought. I had forgotten about the two thugs who had tried to rob me in the park the night before. So much had happened since then that it seemed longer ago.

"Who's scheduled for today?" I asked.

Norma tapped a pencil against her lips and thought. "Allison and Dalia," Norma responded.

'No, Allison won't be in, her mother is sick. Can you call Emily and see if she can come in?"

"Sure thing."

I started toward my office, paused, and turned back. "Oh, and give that kid a call who filled out an application the other day. See if he wants to wash dishes. There's a stack of applications under the bar; his should be in there. Also, look through them and hire another waitress."

"Anything else, Your Highness?"

"Yeah. Don't disturb me."

I went on down the hall to my office.

I closed the door behind me and took a seat on the leather sofa across from my desk. I put my head on the armrest and fell asleep.

*****

I was having a dream about Evan Walsh when my cell phone woke me up. In the dream I was standing next to a hospital bed holding Evan's hand. Doctors and nurses moved about the room in slow motion, their scrubs were stained in blood. None of them seemed to be doing anything other than trying to look busy. A nurse walked behind me and whispered, "I'm sorry."

"Sorry about what?" I asked.

A doctor standing on the other side of the bed looked up at me and slowly shook his head. "I'm so sorry," he said.

"Sorry?" I screaming now. "Sorry about what? What are you sorry about?"

The beeping of the heart monitor slowly turned into the ringing of my cell phone and I opened my eyes.

"Hello?" I said.

"Cole?" June asked.

I cleared my throat. "Yes."

"Oh, it didn't sound like you."

"I fell asleep. What time is it?"

"A little after three."

I sat up on the couch. "What's going on?"

"I was just getting ready to drive down to West Palm to see my sister and I wanted to call you first. How're Lynn and the kids doing?"

"Good, I guess. I haven't heard from anyone. I'll give Allison a call in a bit."

"Are they letting Lynn go home today?"

"As far as I know. Are you coming home tonight or are you staying at your sisters?"

"I might just stay there. I'll call you tomorrow. Maybe we can get together tomorrow night."

"That sounds good."

"Bye, Cole."

"Bye."

I hung up my cell and dialed Kelly's number.

"Hello?" Kelly answered.

"Hey, where are you?"

"Sitting at your bar. Where are you?"

"In my office. I'll be right out … oh, and Kelly?"

"Yeah?"

"I'm sorry."

There was a pause and then Kelly asked, "Sorry about what?"

"Exactly," I said.

Chapter Twenty-Seven

Kelly left the bar around seven-thirty. I made sure I only had two drinks while he was there; I wanted to keep my head clear. I puttered around the bar until eight thirty waiting for the sun to go down and then went to my office.

My shoulder holster hung on a coat hook on the back of my office door. It had hung there for a long time. I put it on over my T-shirt and then went to my desk. I opened the bottom desk drawer and pulled out the lock box where I kept my Smith and Wesson .357 revolver and an old pair of handcuffs. I opened the box, pulled out the weapon, and checked the cylinder. I slid the pistol into the holster and secured it. There was a flannel shirt draped over the back of my chair; I grabbed it and slipped it on. I picked up the handcuffs and slid them into my back pocket.

I flipped off the light and shut the office door behind me and went to the kitchen.

"I'm taking off, Leon," I said.

Leon glanced over at me standing in the middle of the kitchen. "You taking that cannon with you?" he asked.

"It's that noticeable?" I asked.

"It is to me. Most people wouldn't notice it, of course most people haven't been shot with it."

"Sorry, Leon."

"I know."

I turned and left the kitchen. As I walked across the park toward my truck I thought about the boys who tried to rob me the night before. I wondered if anyone would try it tonight. I would truly feel sorry for anyone who did. I also thought about my apology to Leon. He didn't ask what I was sorry about, because he knew why I was sorry. The only reason you wouldn't ask is because you already knew. *What did June already know?* I wondered.

I climbed in my truck and drove to Subway. It was too dark to see the blood stain as I walked across the parking lot toward the rear entrance. I pulled open the door and walked down the hallway past the restrooms.

When Jimmy Bertran saw me round the corner his face turned a funny color—not white, but more an off-white.

I walked up to the counter, past the three people waiting in line. "Can I speak to you outside for a minute, Jimmy?"

"What now?" he asked.

"Right now, Jimmy."

Jimmy looked to his coworkers and shrugged his shoulders letting them know he had no idea what was going on. "I'll be right back," he informed them.

Jimmy led the way back down the hall, out the door, down the steps, and into the parking lot. Part of me thought he might run the second he opened the door, but it didn't happen.

"Which car is yours, Jimmy," I asked as I scanned the dimly lit lot.

Jimmy pointed. "The Malibu over there."

I motioned toward the car and started walking. "Come on."

Jimmy followed. "What's going on?"

When we arrived at Jimmy's vehicle I turned and positioned him between me and the car. He was starting to look a little more nervous. I put my hands on my hips which pulled back my unbuttoned shirt and revealed the grip of my weapon. Jimmy glanced down at the big gun and then back at me.

"If I look in your trunk, Jimmy, will I find a bat, or a crowbar, or maybe a metal pipe?"

Jimmy smiled nervously. "What do you mean? You can't just look in my trunk without a warrant."

"A warrant? Only cops need a warrant, Jimmy."

"You are a cop."

"No, I'm not. I'm a retired cop."

"What's the difference?" Jimmy pulled a pack of cigarettes from his front pocket and I slapped it out of his hand.

"Retired cops are far more dangerous," I told him.

"Hey! What are you doing, man?" He bent to pick up the cigarettes. I grabbed the front of his shirt and shoved him back against the car.

"Who paid you and Freddie Underwood to kill Evan Walsh?" I asked.

He tried to look shocked that I would even ask such a question. "I don't know what you're talking about," he said.

I kept a hold of him with my left hand and reached inside my shirt with my right, grabbing the grip of my pistol. Jimmy's eyes widened as he watched the six inch barrel leave its holster. "You can't do this," he said.

I shoved the barrel up under his chin. "I'm only going to ask you one more time, Jimmy. Who asked you and Freddie to kill Evan Walsh?" He started to open his mouth. "Think about what you're going to say before you say it, Jimmy. It better be what I want to hear."

"It was her, man. It was his wife. She gave us ten grand. I didn't want to do it. Freddie said he would kill me too, and keep all the money for himself if I didn't help him."

I applied more pressure, pushing the gun deeper into his chin. "How did you help him?"

"I drove out to the house Walsh was showing that night. His old lady gave us the address. Then I followed him here. I called Freddie when we were almost here. Walsh went in and got a sandwich and when he came out I ran up behind him and stuck him."

"Where was Freddie?" I could feel my face reddening, and I was now speaking through clenched teeth.

"He came out the back door, he grabbed the knife he had hidden behind the counter. Walsh turned and tried to run back inside but Freddie got him in the gut. He kept fighting us, and we just kept stabbing him. When we were sure he was dead, I drove to Freddie's trailer and changed my clothes and Freddie called 911."

"How did you know Walsh would come here?"

"His old lady told him to come here."

I put my gun away. "Why did she want him dead?" I asked.

"She caught him screwing around with an old girlfriend. She said it was someone he had a kid with years ago. I guess her and this other woman used to be friends or something."

I felt nauseous and the hair on my neck and arms stood on end. "Why did you kill Freddie?"

"He wouldn't pay me. I went to his trailer to get my money and he would only give me half of what I had coming. I told him he better give it to me. He just laughed at me said, 'If you don't like it, go to the cops.' He kept a bat next to his front door. When he turned around, I picked it up and hit him as hard as I could. He fell on the floor and I just kept hitting him. I looked all over his trailer but I couldn't find the rest of the money."

"Where's the bat?"

"It's in my trunk."

"The knives?"

"Trunk."

"Give me your car keys."

Jimmy reached in his front pocket to retrieve the keys and handed them to me. I unlocked his driver's side door and shoved the keys in my pocket. "Get in," I said.

Jimmy climbed into the driver's seat and I cuffed his hands to the steering wheel.

"What are you doing, man?" Jimmy asked.

"Shut up, Jimmy," I said, and pulled out my cell phone. I dialed Tommy Franklin's number.

"Hello?" Tommy said.

"Tommy, it's Cole."

"Hey, Cole. What's going on?"

"You know the parking lot where Evan Walsh was murdered?"

"Yes. Why?"

"There's a kid here who's having some car trouble."

"And?"

"I was wondering if you could drive over here and give him a hand."

"What the hell you want me to do about it? Tell him to call the fuckin' Triple A."

"Tommy, I wouldn't ask you to come over if I didn't think it was important. Now, when you get here, the trunk will be open."

"The trunk?"

"Yeah, the trunk, Tommy. Look in the trunk when you get here." I hung up the phone.

"You're just gonna leave me here?" Jimmy asked.

I reached inside and pushed the button to open the trunk. "Yeah, and if you honk that horn or try to get anyone's attention, I'll find you and I'll blow your goddamn head off. Ya got it?" I took his keys out of my pocket and tossed them in the trunk.

Jimmy shook his head yes and I slammed the car door.

I waited next to Jimmy's car for about fifteen minutes. Then I got in my truck and drove to June's.

Chapter Twenty-Eight

When I pulled up in front of June's home I saw her car parked in the driveway. She had decided to come home from her sister's after all. I pulled to the curb and shut off the engine. Her blinds were open and the living room was lit. Wealthy people love to leave the blinds open and their lights on after dark—that way you can see what they have and you don't. June had no idea she was about to lose it all.

I knocked on the door and June answered soon after. "Cole," she said surprised.

"June," I replied. "You decided to come home tonight."

"Yes. I was going to call you."

"Can I come in?"

"Of course." She pulled the door open a little farther and I walked in past her.

"Is everything okay?" she asked.

Halfway down the hall I turned around and put my hands on my hips. "Detective Franklin is with Jimmy Bertan as we speak." The expression on her face didn't change. She was good. "The bat he used to kill Freddie Underwood and the knives they used to murder Evan are in the trunk of his car."

June looked at the floor and shook her head. "I told them to get rid of the knives. Stupid kids."

"Is C.J. Evan's son?"

Her eyes slowly rose to meet mine. "Yes."

I ran my fingers through my hair and scratched the back of my head. I felt like I was going to puke. "How long have you known?"

"I've known about their affair since the beginning, but I didn't find out about C.J. until a few weeks before Evan's death."

"You mean a few weeks before you had him murdered."

"I found Lynn's number on his cell phone and confronted him. He said nothing was going on, but I knew better. I followed him out to her house two different times when he said he had to show a house. We fought and he finally admitted to me that C.J. was his."

"Does Lynn know that you know about C.J.?" I asked.

"I don't think so."

As I walked past June on my way to the door, she grabbed my arm. "Please, Cole, don't be angry with me. I really do like you. What we have means something to me."

"No it doesn't, June. What we *had* was just some sick way of you getting back at Evan and Lynn." I pulled loose from her grip and continued out the door. "It's only a matter of time until Jimmy Bertran gives you up. I figure Franklin will be here in the next couple of hours. It might look better for you if you turn yourself in."

As I backed out of June's driveway she just stood in the doorway staring at me. I thought about going back to the bar and having a few drinks, but I drove home instead.

When I pulled into my driveway the headlights flashed across the front of my apartment and I could see Angel sitting on the stoop. *Two nights in a row. Must be trouble in paradise.*

I walked up to the front door. Angel was sitting on the concrete with her knees pulled up in front of her and her head down. I stopped and stood over her with my arms folded across my chest. She sniffed and looked up at me. I reached out and she took my hand; I helped her to her feet.

"Waiting for me?" I asked.

She didn't answer.

I got her into the house and she sat down on the couch. When I flipped on the living room light I could see her purple and swollen eye. There was a bruise on the left side of her chin and her lip was swollen and bloody. "Jesus Christ," I said. "When did this happen?"

"Earlier today," she replied. "I'm so stupid. I try my hardest not to make him mad but I always do something stupid. It's not his fault, Daddy. I just make him so angry."

Her words felt like a knife in my heart. How did this happen? How did we get here? How could my little girl be beaten by some piece of shit like Ted Hale and feel that it was her fault? What did I do wrong? What could I do to make it right?

"Let's get you cleaned up," I said.

I went with Angel into the bathroom. She sat on the edge of the tub as I wiped the dried blood from her face. I wiped the dirt from her knees.

"How did you get here?" I asked.

"I walked."

"All the way from Ted's place?" I looked down at her feet; she wasn't wearing any shoes.

"Yes," she replied.

I lifted her leg and wiped the dirt from the bottoms of her feet. "Do you want to take a shower?" I asked.

"No, I just want to change my clothes and go to bed."

I tucked Angel into bed, pulled the covers up to her chin, and kissed her on the forehead. "Good night, princess."

"Good night, Daddy."

I went into the kitchen and heated up a cup of that morning's coffee. I took it into the living room and sat in front of the television for about an hour watching two old episodes of some early nineties sitcom; I'm not sure which one. My mind was on other things.

I put my empty coffee cup in the sink and looked in on Angel; she was sound asleep. I felt my cell phone vibrate in my pocket and looked at the screen; it was June. I tossed the cell on the couch and walked outside. I climbed in my truck, and backed out of the driveway.

Chapter Twenty-Nine

It was a little after midnight when I pulled to the edge of Oleander Avenue and shut off my engine. I got out of my truck and walked about fifty yards to the dirt driveway where Ted Hale's Plymouth Duster was parked. I placed the palm of my hand on the hood as I walked by; it was cold.

I continued up the walkway to the front door. With my flannel shirt between my hand and the knob, I turned it. The door was unlocked; I slowly pushed it open. I walked into the kitchen and flipped on the ceiling light. Instantly small cockroaches scurried under the refrigerator, a noisy avocado relic plastered with beer coupons and attorney magnets. A Lynyrd Skynyrd tune wafted from somewhere in the rear of the house. The house looked like a cluttered Goodwill showroom and smelled of garbage that hadn't been taken to the curb in weeks. I reached inside my shirt and pulled out my .357. I peered into the living room and saw no one. The walls of each room were covered with old wallpaper from the sixties, and the nicotine-stained moldings, once white, were a sticky shade of yellow.

I went down the hall and opened the first door I came to. It was a bedroom. The same black man who was passed out on a sleeping bag in the drug house on Twenty-Eighth Street was now lying in bed asleep. He rolled over and faced the wall. I pulled the door shut and went on.

The door to the next room was open. Ted Hale lay in bed on top of the blankets, wearing only boxer shorts. I stepped into the room; the floorboards creaked beneath me.

"Hey," I said quietly. "Hey!" a little louder.

There was no movement or response from Ted. I put my gun back in the holster and walked up beside the bed. I nudged Ted's shoulder with my fist; he still didn't move. I watched his chest rise and fall as he lay there in his drug-induced slumber. I picked up the pillow that lay beside him, covered his face with it, and applied the pressure I thought was necessary to stop his breathing.

The room flashed white and I felt a sudden pain in the back of my head. I fell forward onto the bed and rolled off onto my back. Standing above me was Ted's roommate. He seemed to be much larger with a shovel raised above his head than he did getting his beauty sleep.

I reached into my shirt, pulled out my weapon, and fired twice into his chest. The shovel fell from his grip and he stumbled backwards and fell to the floor.

Ted sat up in bed, turned toward me as I was getting to my feet.

"What are you doing?" he asked. He scooted backwards until his back was against the wall.

I trained the Smith and Wesson on his head.

"Please, don't," Ted pleaded. "Take anything you want. Please, don't hurt me."

"Ted," I said calmly, "I just want you to know that this isn't my fault, and I know you try your hardest not to, but sometimes you just make me so angry."

I fired one round into Ted Hale's forehead.

As I strolled back down Oleander Avenue toward my truck I thought about how shitty the last two days had gone. I figured things might even get a little bit shittier in the next few days, but as for tonight, I felt a little better knowing that Ted Hale had abused his last little princess.

The End

ALSO BY RODNEY RIESEL

Sleeping Dogs Lie
From the Tales of Dan Coast

A mystery set in the Florida Keys follows Dan Coast, an unlicensed private detective of sorts, as he is hired to find the missing boyfriend of a woman who herself soon ends up missing. When someone from the woman's past unexpectedly shows up at Dan's home, with a story of faked deaths and missing life insurance money; Dan along with his sidekick Red set out to find the money, and the woman.

ISBN: 978-0-9883503-0-4

Ocean Floors
From the Tales of Dan Coast

The second installment in the Dan Coast series, Ocean Floors, is a tale of mystery and possible romance when a chance meeting with a beautiful young woman leads Dan and his trusted sidekick Red down a road of murder and kidnapping. Join Dan and Red as they try to solve the murder while searching for a missing friend.

ISBN: 978-0-9894877-0-2

North Murder Beach
A Jake Stellar Novel

The first installment of the story of North Myrtle Beach police detective, Jake Stellar. The spring bike rallies have ended, the spring breakers have all gone back to school, and the summer tourist season is a few weeks away. What better time for a police officer to take a nice quiet relaxing week off from work? That's what Jake Stellar had in mind. That is until someone from his past resurfaces to remind him of a terrible secret he has spent years trying to forget. In North Murder Beach, a story of revenge, Jake is unwillingly and violently forced to confront his secret from his past.

ISBN: 978-0-9894877-1-9

The Coast of Christmas Past
From the Tales of Dan Coast

Coast of Christmas Past is the third book in the Dan Coast series of books. Dan Coast is all set to spend Christmas just the same way he has every year for the past few years; alone and drunk. But when uninvited, unexpected guests arrive and throw a wrench into his holiday plans he is forced to sober up (slightly), and throw on a smile. Just when it seems nothing else could go wrong, a close friend is injured in what appears, to the police, to be a drug deal gone bad. Dan Coast and his sidekick, Red jump into action to find the truth while their friend lies unconscious in the hospital.

ISBN: 978-0-9894877-3-3

The Man in Room Number Four
The Dunquin Cove Series

When a mysterious stranger arrives in the small coastal town of Dunquin Cove, Maine it appears as though Claire and her young son, Mica's prayers have been answer.

But who is he, and why is he really here? Join Claire and her guests at the Colsome House Bed and Breakfast as they piece together the mystery of the Man in Room Number Four.

ISBN: 978-0-9894877-2-6

Ship of Fools
From the Tales of Dan Coast

Ship of Fools is the fourth book in The Tales of Dan Coast series and begins where Coasts of Christmas Past left off. Find out how Dan deals with the death of a young friend, while looking into the disappearance of a new friend's sister. Join Dan, Red, and Skip as they fumble their way through a new mystery.

ISBN: 978-0-9894877-4-0

Beach Shoot
A Jake Stellar Series

It's a beautiful Sunday morning in North Myrtle Beach and Emily Bowen, a wife and mother of four, lies dying on the beach. Jake Stellar returns in Beach Shoot, a new mystery by Rodney Riesel.

Beach Shoot is the second Jake Stellar book and sequel to the Amazon Best Seller North Murder Beach. In Beach Shoot, Jake finds himself teamed up with the most unlikely of partners, his nemesis and fellow detective Avis Lint. Join Jake and Avis as they piece together the clues in this thrilling new mystery.

ISBN: 978-0-9894877-5-7

Return to Dunquin Cove
The Dunquin Cove Series

It's been almost six months since the day ex-hitman, Ben Dunning turned up in Dunquin Cove, Maine, not knowing where or who he was. He's lived a quiet, peaceful life in the small town, but now his old life is calling him back. As Ben plans a trip to Boston in search of his past, little does he know that trouble is brewing in Dunquin Cove. Two strangers have arrived with the promise of safety and security. Join Ben and the people of Dunquin Cove as they band together to prove they can take care of themselves and their town.

ISBN: 978-0-9894877-7-1

Double Trouble
From the Tales of Dan Coast

Shortly after Walter and Warren Bowman arrive in Key West in search of a sister they never knew they had, Warren disappears. With nowhere else to turn, Walter enlists the help of Dan Coast. Join Dan as he and sidekick Red Baxter search for the missing Bowman family members, while dealing with the fallout of an ongoing case.

ISBN: 978-0-9894877-9-5

When Death Returns
A Jake Stellar Series

Has a serial killer from the past returned to North Myrtle Beach? Jake Stellar is back in When Death Returns. Join Jake and his partner Avis Lint in this exciting third installment of the Jake Stellar series as they investigate a homicide that eerily echoes the past.

ISBN: 978-0-9971149-0-4

From Here to There: A Collection of Short Stories

Within this book is a collection of short stories I have written over the past few years. The stories were mostly inspired by trips I've taken, places I've stayed, and conversations I've overheard from Maine to Florida. Although these stories differ from ones I have released in the past, I hope you will enjoy reading them as much as I enjoyed writing them.

ISBN: 978-0-9971149-1-1

Most Likely to Die
From the Tales of Dan Coast

How does someone with no enemies end up murdered? That's for Dan Coast and his sidekick Red Baxter to find out. Join Dan and Red, along with Skip Stoner and Dan's childhood hero, former astronaut, Kip Larson as they piece together the clues that may free an innocent man. In this action packed, sixth installment of The Tales of Dan Coast Series, Dan digs into a wrongly accused man's past and finds out he may not be so innocent.

ISBN: 978-0-9971149-2-8

The Obedience of Fools
A Jake Stellar Series

Join Detective Jake Stellar and his partner, Detective Avis Lint in this fast paced, North Myrtle Beach based Jake Stellar Series. In this fourth installment, The Obedience of Fools, Jake and Avis butt heads with some of The Grand Strand's elite as they try to uncover a secret that may hold the answer to a string of recent homicides.

ISBN: 978-0-9971149-3-5

Deadly Moves
From the Tales of Dan Coast

Dan Coast has finally bought himself a new car, well, new to him. But when he returns to pick up his new ride, he gets an unwanted surprise. In Deadly Moves, the seventh installment in the Tales of Dan Coast Series, we also see the return of Officer Mel Gormin. Join Dan, Red, Mel, and Skip as they do their best to solve the murder of an elderly couple while working as bodyguards to a young starlet who is visiting Key West.

ISBN: 978-0-9971149-4-2